To Big Frank and to Lady Mac
—and especially to Sonrisal

THEIR MAN IN
THE WHITE HOUSE

CHAPTER ONE

You try to figure it. Exactly one month to the day I had been sitting at a typewriter staring at twenty-one words. The words were staring back at me. They said, "The trouble with most of our corner stores these days is that they are located in the middle of the block."

One lousy paragraph and it had taken me half an hour to write it. Half an hour and it wasn't any good. Carano was going to take one look at it and say, "What the hell?" Then we were going to have an argument. It's bright, maybe, but what does it say, kid? What does it *say*?

So it was a relief when the telephone rang and it was Morley. "I need you," Morley had said.

"When?"

"Now."

"Okay," I had told him, and I had hung up, and I had left the paper stuffed in the typewriter. "The trouble with most of our corner stores ..."

I got a kick out of leaving it just like that. Carano was going to come around asking for the story, reminding me that I had a deadline, for Chrissakes, and he was going to find the sheet of paper, but not me, and he was going to say, "What the hell ... ?"

Exactly one month to the day and now I was a couple of thousand miles away feeling my body relax in the new warmth. The sun had finally made it over the hill on my left. A few wavering, tentative, exploratory shafts. A kiss and a promise.

I finished off my can of beer, took a last drag on my Viceroy, reached for the rifle and edged forward as far as I dared. I don't like heights and this was pretty high. At least three hundred feet and a sheer drop.

The riders were perhaps a mile away. Six ants winding along the valley floor. A small ragged column moving against a vast and color-shot backdrop. Half a dozen tiny figures plodding across the tacky paint of the dawn's new masterpiece. Expected and welcome guests but nevertheless intruders blaspheming my private and very special view of the awakening day.

It was a view that persisted in filling me with wonder. The wide sweep of the valley floor. The softly rising foothills of the Sierra Madres. The looming jagged hump of Mount Alamos. The distant town so sparkling white, the ground cover all green and brown and yellow and gold, the cloudless sky as blue as the sky gets anywhere. The converging tributaries of El Fuerte River. The old road that was once the Camino Real.

That kept me happy until they were close enough.

Marshall was leading the pack. Not that it was his idea. Rather it was the horse's. He came out from behind a line of trees riding very awkwardly, bouncing in the saddle, fighting the animal, and from the expression on his face—sort of screwed up and his mouth a tight line—he wasn't enjoying himself at all. The way he was bouncing, I couldn't keep his head in the scope for more than a split second, but every time he came back into view, he had the same expression. A man in pain.

He was sure hard to figure sometimes. Davis Berwick Marshall, electronics genius, multimillionaire, one of the nation's most unusual and successful businessmen, darling of the conservative set and big business, and a candidate—very shortly—for the presidency of the United States.

If he couldn't ride, if he didn't like riding, what the hell was he doing down there, making like Roy Rogers? Why wasn't he doing something he really enjoyed? He certainly had the money to do anything his heart desired. His holdings in just his electronics firm, Marshall-Kramer, Inc., totaled 4,120,700 shares, and they were worth $310,688,100 at last week's stock market closing.

If it was me, I decided, following him with the rifle, watching him bounce in the scope, the geography and the activity would be somewhat different. I wouldn't be bumbling along at eight o'clock of a crisp February morning through cactus and brambles on a ranch trail winding out of a sleepy little town such as Alamos. I'd still be between the clean white sheets of a king-sized bed in the most expensive hotel in Acapulco. And I sure as hell wouldn't be riding no horse.

But then to each his own and I had to admit there was a certain attraction to Alamos—especially if you were a nut on history. Francisco Vasquez de Coronado, when he set out in 1540 to search for the Seven Golden Cities of Cibola, camped on the present site of Alamos. In 1630 the Jesuits built an adobe mission for the Indians on the present location of the roughhewn but elegant old stone church that is the town's focal point. Discovery of the Mines of the Promentorios, in 1683, marks the actual founding of the place, and a baptism on May 12, 1685, starts the official records.

The mines made a lot of people rich before they petered out. There were years when Alamos shipped out more bars of silver than all the other mining areas in the whole Kingdom of Spain. Legend says one of the mine owners laid a sidewalk of silver bars from his casa to the church for his daughter's wedding. And they still look for buried treasure in the thick adobe walls of the old ruins that mingle with the magnificent restored casas.

Perhaps it was the reminders of the fabulous riches of that extraordinary silver strike that attracted Marshall to Alamos. The mine owners, in their day, were as rich as kings, and everywhere you looked there was evidence of the splendor in which they lived. Or perhaps it was just the town's historical significance—the singular link it had with the settling of California. In 1775, Captain Juan Bautista de Anza and 177 persons set out from Alamos, bent on providing a white population for Alta California. They landed at what is now San Francisco, and on September 17, 1776, dedicated the Presidio. A few years later, a second party of settlers was recruited in the Mexican states of Sinaloa and Sonora, and forty-six persons from Alamos joined that group, which founded Los Angeles on September 4, 1781.

But what did it matter? It was the man who was important. Not the place he chose to spend his winter vacations. I pulled my mind away from the town and back to the handsome face bouncing in the scope of my rifle. Davis Berwick Marshall. Quite a success story.

He got his first taste of electronics as an enlisted man in the Army in World War II. Once out of the service he quickly picked up an engineering degree on the GI Bill of Rights and then started his electronics company in a San Diego garage with a $2,200 stake. With his inventive genius it was only a few short years before the company became one of the world's largest manufacturers of electronic devices of all kinds. In the postwar era of computers, television and solid-state circuitry, Marshall-Kramer, Inc., showed the way, and now its sales had grown to more than $300 million annually.

For a moment I almost wished I could trade places with him. To be that well known, powerful and influential. To have all that lovely, lovely money. To be able to go anywhere and do anything. I asked myself again why he had chosen Alamos for his retreat. Why a sleepy little town in the mountains, a place where time stood still, a relic of the distant past that was falsely advertised as a Government Colonial Monument?

The damn town. My mind kept going back to it. The city fathers had a good thing going for them and they knew it. They had decreed that the physical aspects should remain unaltered.

Arcades could not give way to glass fronts, cobblestones to black-top, nor wrought-iron corner lamps to neon signs. Walk down the narrow streets and except for the cars and the television antennas you were back in the eighteenth century.

An old town, a sleepy town, a quiet town—and perhaps it really was the answer for a man who has everything. Marshall, at any rate, kept coming back, spending a month each winter in a restored casa that once served as the home of a wealthy mine owner's mistress. One month in a place where time stood still apparently was enough to repair his inner mechanisms and send him back renewed and replenished to the stresses and strains of the atomic era.

To hell with it. I told myself to stop arguing Marshall's choice. He liked the place, and that was the important thing, wasn't it? He liked the old ways, and the complete tranquillity, and the almost perfect climate. The bright, sunny days. The cool, crisp nights ...

Jesus. I was starting to like the place myself, and that would never do, I thought. I blinked and pushed my eye back against the scope. Marshall's big proud bay had drawn up. The torture of the ride had momentarily stopped. My candidate for the presidency had a big grin on his handsome face.

I had him now. The scope's cross hairs were dead on. Right between those marvelously deep liquid green eyes.

I pulled the trigger.

CHAPTER TWO

They had been a good half mile away from the caravan. I made it there well before they arrived. I was sitting on the steps, my breath back to normal, cleaning the rifle, when they came riding into the clearing. Marshall was again leading the pack. That big bay, soon as he gets his head, he's sure a traveling man. Some day I'm going to own a horse like him.

"Buenos días," Marshall shouted.

I waved hello, put the rifle aside and ambled down to hold the bay. Marshall, as usual, was very relieved to get out of the saddle, to get his feet firmly planted on the good mother earth. The bay was damp and smelled very horsey. Marshall smelled too. Of soap, and talc, and skin bracer. A strong smell and an expensive one. He smiled his much photographed smile.

"Any luck this morning?"

"No," I said. "He didn't show up this morning. I must have spooked him good yesterday."

I had been waiting on the butte for a big buck that had discovered my water hole in the arroyo winding down from the hills back of my caravan. It had taken me two days of blood, sweat and tears to dam up the arroyo and trap a bit of water from the occasional winter rains. Damn hard work, but worth it, though. I had already taken a couple of small bucks and there isn't any better eating than the deer around Alamos. Firm, tender, sweet and no gamy taste. They don't grow to much of a haunch normally. About the size of a greyhound and twice as fast. The big buck was special. I was happy in a way that he hadn't come back.

"We flushed a lot of doves coming up," Marshall said. "White wings. The sesame fields are loaded with them. You ought to try your hand there."

I made a face. "All feathers."

The others pulled in. Tyler, Sam Oppman, Ace King, Maggie Hilton and a new addition to the riding academy. Marshall's daughter. As she swung out of the saddle, she got her first look at me, and her face went very hard and white. It was as if someone had slapped her unexpectedly and she still hadn't figured out how to react.

I couldn't figure it either. The girls are supposed to smile prettily when they first view the Sparrow profile. They are very definitely not supposed to go hard and white.

Marshall was aware of the look on her face and he seemed to be making a silent apology to her. It was really a strange moment, she staring at me in shock and disbelief, and he appearing to beg that she understand. A weird moment and then it quickly passed.

"This is the little lady I've been bragging about," Marshall said. "Lisa, I'd like you to meet the town's only hippie, Charlie Sparrow."

"Hi," Lisa said. She turned away from me.

Marshall had a right to brag. I had seen photographs of her but meeting her was something else. She had that sort of flawless beauty you seldom get to see in the flesh. Her father's marvelously deep liquid green eyes. Finely chiseled nose with just enough pug to avoid being regal. A wide, full, slightly pouting mouth glistening with a hot wet invitation. Very straight, very strong, very white teeth. Hair the color of ripe bananas. Right now it was worn in a bun. It would be worn other ways.

"The coffee's waiting," I told Marshall. I led his bay over to the hitch beside the caravan. The others tied their own.

"What do you think of this damn thing?" Marshall asked Lisa.

"It's different," she admitted. "What is it? One of the props left over from *Tobacco Road?*"

This in reference to my caravan. It's sort of hard to describe. You know what a gypsy's wagon looks like? Well, my caravan is in that style, only much more hip, and it is built on the deck of an old flatbed Dodge truck. It sits very high, the front end jutting over the cab of the truck, and it is quite boxy, being designed for comfort, not speed. Rustic as all hell. Dark green Duroid sheeting on the outer walls. Tar and gravel for the curved half-moon roof. Some rather nice touches like a big skylight and narrow stained-glass windows and oil lanterns hanging at the elaborately carved door. Different, Lisa had said, and that was the whole idea, little lady.

I bowed and motioned her up the fold-down steps. "My humble home."

She entered dubiously and her slow passage treated my nose to yet another aroma. Unlike Marshall's, it wasn't a strong smell, but it was still expensive. Damn expensive. Like everything about her. Cashmere sweater, raw silk blouse, fine wool slacks stuffed carelessly into soft leather boots. Some outfit for riding through brambles and cactus.

I followed the pack in and turned up the propane under the coffee pot. Maggie hadn't sat down. She moved over beside me. "May I help?"

"Sure," I said. I slipped past her and pointed to the row of white enamel mugs sitting on the sideboard. "Soon as it perks, serve, okay?"

Maggie, I feared, was getting designs on me, and I was doing my best to stay very loose and plainly free. Normally I would have had her in the lower bunk long ago. She was recently divorced, she was down for the winter, she was trying to forget, and she hadn't found anybody to forget with. Alamos suffers from a severe shortage of youngish gringos. It's mainly a hideaway for the elderly and the rich. The rich aren't young. Or at least not very often.

"How's the book coming?" Marshall asked.

"So-so," I lied. "You want to see the latest?"

"You don't think I ride out here just to drink your lousy coffee?"

"Help yourself."

He crossed eagerly to my desk. There were twenty-two fresh pages of manuscript sitting beside my Royal Safari portable. He picked them up, returned to his easy chair, and made a production of putting on his horn-rimmed glasses.

I took a bench across from Lisa. She was just getting a cigarette going. Tyler was lighting it for her. Well, now, thanks loads, Tyler.

"Nice layout you've got here," Oppman told me. It was his first visit to the caravan and he seemed suitably impressed. He ran a practiced finger over the metalwork in the stained-glass window next to his head. "You build it yourself?"

"No."

"Your idea?"

"Yes."

"Never saw anything like it before."

I shrugged. Oppman was quite a talker. If he got going on the caravan, there would be no stopping him, and I wanted to make the most of this first meeting with Lisa.

"When did you get down?" I asked her.

She regarded me through a curl of cigarette smoke. "Last night."

"Did it cost much?" Oppman asked.

"No," I said. That was too abrupt. I turned back to him. "Much less than the average camper."

His eyes lit up. "No kidding?"

Ace King laughed. "You thinking of getting one?"

"Not really," Oppman said. "But it makes good sense. This you can at least stand up in." He returned his attention to me. "You say less, huh?"

I nodded. Oppman's concern over the height was amusing. He was one of those very tiny Jews. He could practically stand up under a table.

"This is awfully good," Marshall said.

"Thanks," I told him. It had better be good. It had been written by a winner of the Pulitzer Prize for Fiction.

"Really," Marshall said. "It's quite well done. I don't know how you can be so consistent."

"Thanks," I repeated. It was easy. The book was written. I took two dozen pages or so out of the safe every night and put them beside the typewriter.

"Charlie is a genius," Tyler said. He obviously didn't mean it.

"How do you like it?" Maggie asked no one in particular. The caravan was filled with the coffee's aroma.

It took us a while to get all that sorted out. By then Ace King was on his favorite subject. Fishing.

"Dutch and I were at the beach day before yesterday," he was telling Tyler. "The Sierras are really running. We got thirty-two."

"Ick," Maggie said. "Who cleans them?"

Ace King accepted his coffee from her. "We give 'em away. There's plenty of Mexican families around who can use 'em."

"So can I," Oppman said. "Next time you're giving them away, drop a few off at my place, huh?"

"Sure," Ace said. He thought for a moment. "We're going to the dam tomorrow morning. Want to come with us?"

Oppman shook his head.

"You fish?" Tyler asked Lisa.

She waved away some smoke. "Occasionally."

"She's a pro," Marshall reported. He put the manuscript aside regretfully in exchange for the coffee. He still had a couple of pages to go. "You should have seen the marlin she took once off La Paz. It weighed three hundred and twenty-two pounds."

Lisa stubbed out her cigarette. I got a look down her blouse as she leaned forward. They were rather nice specimens. Full, firm, milk-white where the tan ended. She glanced up aware of my attention. Her tongue played thoughtfully with her teeth.

"You want?" Maggie demanded.

I took the coffee. There was cream in it. She must be really sore.

"That's pretty good for a woman," Ace said. He glanced at Marshall. Asking for permission. "Anytime you want to come with me and Dutch, just say the word, miss."

Lisa smiled her thanks. "Perhaps later. I want to rest for a few days first."

"You need it," Marshall agreed indulgently. "You've been on the go far too much these past few months." His eye caught mine. "I had a tough time getting her down here. She's never liked Alamos. Not enough males around."

Maggie's problem. I tested my coffee. It was as sweet as syrup. Oh, she was sore, all right.

"Enjoy it while it lasts," Lisa said dryly. "I won't be hanging around very long. Nothing has changed as far as I can see."

Really?

"Give it a chance," Tyler said. His grin was almost a leer. Way to go, Tyler. You're a cool one, you are.

Maggie sat down beside me. She edged along the bench possessively. "Like your coffee?"

"It's okay."

"I made it just the way you like it."

"So I see."

Oppman was examining the floor of the caravan. He ran a fingernail along a crack. "What is it? Oak?"

I nodded.

"How long you had it?"

"A couple three years."

"Nice," he said. He looked around for other wonders.

"He's thinking of getting one," Ace laughed.

I tried once more with Lisa. "How long do you intend to stay?"

She shrugged. The green eyes were flat and bored. "I'm not sure."

Tyler had his lighter out while she was still thinking about having a second cigarette.

I took one of my Viceroys. I'd been trying to cut down, get back to a pack a day, and this was ahead of my schedule. I needed it, though. I was batting zero.

"At least a week," Marshall said. He waited until she had her cigarette lit. "You promised me that. Remember?"

"It can be awfully dull around here," Maggie said.

"Nonsense," Marshall told her. He finished his coffee and returned to the manuscript. I watched him out of the corner of my eye. He had three pages to go. Not two.

"It depends on what you're interested in," Ace announced ponderously. "Now, you take that Alice Shafter. When she first came down here—what is it, five, six years ago?—she said she liked to go out of her mind. No movies. No television. No telephones to yak on."

Oppman was working his way up the walls. "In other words, paradise," he said. He looked at me. "You got insulation in here?"

"Rock wool."

"Just a few months changed all that," Ace said. "You should see her now. A real little homebody. Her casa is a palace and there isn't a garden in the world that's better than the one she's got."

Marshall peered over the manuscript. "You, sir, are showing a dangerous interest in the widow Shafter ...."

Ace reddened slightly.

"Does the job?" Oppman asked.

I nodded.

"Yes, and she's a good cook, too, damn it," Ace said, recovering nicely. He pointed an accusing finger at Maggie. "Get yourself other interests," he ordered.

"I'll be gone before a garden sprouts," she told him. She let the statement hang there wistfully. Nobody called her on it. Poor Maggie.

"Lighter than sawdust," Oppman observed knowingly.

The talk went on like that, three or four conversations going on at once, with Marshall making asides over the manuscript, and Tyler bird-dogging Lisa. I gave up on her for the moment and concentrated on watching Marshall's reaction to my latest offering.

The interest he was showing was typical of the man. He was intrigued with it now, perhaps, but in the beginning, the first time he had come around, he had asked to see it out of kindness. Either that or a wonderful empathy for his fellow-man, be they rich or poor, brilliant or stupid, vastly entertaining or boring as hell.

What else explained his wide choice of riding companions? Normally, a man that rich and famous would be inclined to be choosy, associating only with the people of his own class, but everybody in town—everybody and anybody—was an honorary member of his riding academy.

He was just one of the crowd that got together every morning at the plaza and went bouncing off into the hills. It was a wide-open club. Everybody was welcome to join. The Alamos Dudes.

"You're on the beam, Charles, my boy," Marshall said. He slapped the pages back on the desk. "It's good. Awfully good." He swung around to Lisa. "You want to watch this young fellow. He's going to go places."

"Charlie is a genius," Tyler said.

Lisa slumped down in her chair. She crossed her long legs at the ankle. "When?"

"Soon as this book is published," Marshall said. "One of the best things I've ever read. It's a sure-fire best seller."

"Your first?"

"Of many," Marshall answered for me. He frowned at his daughter. "I told you it was his first ..."

Lisa blew out a long theatrical stream of smoke. "Father's told me all about you, Charlie," she grinned.

"Oh?"

"He says you're one of the best magazine writers in the country. Literally forced me to read some of the cover stories you've written for *Time*. And he's most impressed with the way you've thrown up everything to come down here in your cute little caravan to write the world's greatest novel...." She batted her long eyelashes at me. "It's all just too marvelous for words. Mr. Wonderful."

Marshall's face flushed. It deserved to be red. He had been checking up on me. I had not told him I once worked for *Time*.

"A genius," Tyler said.

Marshall managed a smile. "I guess I have been laying it on pretty thick."

"Keep it up," I said. I stood with my empty coffee cup. "Every little plug counts. Who knows? Maybe golden girl here will buy a copy...."

"What for?" Lisa asked. "I already know the plot. He's told me practically word for word." She laughed a little too loudly. A deep, rich, throaty laugh. "The author did it."

Ace handed me his cup. "What is it? A mystery?"

Tyler giggled.

I took the cups to the sink. Despite Lisa's lack of interest, I felt pretty damn good. Things actually were going better than expected. Marshall, obviously, since he had gone to the trouble of running a check, was thinking of me as a possible member of his campaign staff. And he must want me pretty badly to drag down his daughter as bait. Not that she was being very co-operative. Yet.

"Anybody want seconds?" I asked.

There was a chorus of no's. Some day I must learn how to make coffee.

"It's time we got going," Tyler said. He cracked his head on one of the open beams when he stood up. That would have been done on purpose. To remind Lisa that he was six foot four.

She was up immediately to see if he had hurt himself. "My God! That was an *awful* whack!"

He lowered his curly head for her examination. "Ain't nothing in there to get damaged."

Marshall seemed to be scowling as they clowned through the nurse-patient routine. I moved slightly for a better view and was rewarded with a new insight into the man. That wasn't a scowl. It was a look of burning anger. So he could get like that when he didn't have his own way?

"Who built this for you?" Oppman asked.

"A friend."

"He in the business?"

"No."

Oppman's face fell. "I don't suppose he'd build another?"

"Sorry," I told him. "He just did it for kicks. He's actually very busy with other things now."

Ace punched me playfully on the shoulder. "When you going to use that rod of yours?"

"Pretty soon. The book's almost finished."

"You writer fellows," Ace said. He led the way out the door.

I glanced at my watch. They hadn't been inside for more than half an hour. That God damn Tyler. Every time he sat down it was time he was going. He had the attention span of a grasshopper.

Lisa stopped in front of me. She licked a finger and wiped something off the side of my face. She patted my cheek, green eyes crinkled, pouting lips glistening. "I almost forgot," she said. "You know father's big party tonight? You're my date." She didn't wait for a reply.

"Six o'clock," Marshall said. He was all smiles now. "Come earlier if you want. And keep up the good work. It's terrific. Really terrific."

Tyler didn't look too happy. That didn't worry me a bit. Screw you, Tyler.

"It's been nice," Maggie said. She shook hands formally. She had never done that before.

Oppman was the last to leave. "You wouldn't consider selling, would you?"

"No," I said.

I stood at the top of the steps watching them mount up. Sell the caravan? Sweet Mother of Christ! Morley would kill me.

"Adiós," Marshall said. The big bay took off like a rocket. His master went bumpity-bumpity-bump.

There were only two good riders in the bunch. Tyler, of course. And Lisa.

I waved good-bye and went back into the caravan and poured myself another cup of coffee. Black. No sugar.

I sat down where Lisa had been. There was still a faint trace of her perfume.

There were times, I decided, pulling at the coffee, when you really had to hand it to Morley. The caravan had been his idea. The caravan, the novel, the whole parade. Even the placement. Way back on the ranch at the end of the trail. The easy trail that a rider like Marshall was bound to take quite often.

Often? Hell, he had taken it his first day down, riding out tight-lipped as he had this morning, leading a pack of painfully determined fellow dudes. And when they had come out from behind the line of trees and seen the caravan? Well, if it was just an ordinary camper or house trailer, they might not have paid any attention, but a gypsy caravan perched on the deck of an old flatbed truck is something different. You want to ride over to get a close look at it. You want to get a gander at the character who lives in that.

So they had come riding over. Marshall and Maggie Hilton. H. H. Goding, David Snell and Les Beardsley. It was up to me then and I carried it off rather well. I served them coffee, showed off the caravan, revealed myself as a magazine writer going after the whole ball of wax, and got Marshall more than just a trifle interested in The Book.

Two mornings later he was back. Maggie was with him again and so was H. H. Goding. Snell and Beardsley weren't riding that day but there were some new faces. Tyler, Ace King and Mavis Dampier. I gave Marshall the first eight chapters of the manuscript. I'd appreciate his opinion, I said, and a man like him, who must know a lot of the really big wheels in the publishing business—well, if he thought there was anything to the book, perhaps he would be kind enough to recommend it. Or something.

Marshall had been flattered. He was very large in business and industry, hardly a week went by when he didn't make a million-dollar decision, there was talk of him seeking the presidency of the United States, but no one, apparently, had ever asked his opinion of an unpublished literary effort. This was something different for him. A new avenue for him to explore.

The first eight chapters impressed him. They would have impressed anybody with the slightest appreciation for good writing. They were written, as I've said, by one of the best craftsmen in the business, and his agent was of the opinion that this last effort on his part—he died shortly after completing it—was quite the best he had ever turned out.

Marshall took a paternal interest in the book after that. He rode out almost every morning to read my latest offerings. The way I was supposedly churning it out, an average of two dozen pages a day, all of it great and getting better, provided just the kind of quiet excitement he needed in his otherwise pretty dull routine around Alamos. For a brief period each morning he was a witness to creation.

He hardly ever missed a day. The other riders switched around a lot. Some, like Ace King, were fairly regular, and others, like Beardsley, only came the once. But Marshall rarely missed. Marshall and Maggie Hilton. I forgot about Maggie. She had her hopes and she was consistent.

It must have been somewhere after the first week that Marshall started considering me as a possibility for his campaign staff for the presidency. It was about then that he had first mentioned his daughter, and how anxious he was to get her down, to have her with him at least part of the month he spent every winter in Alamos. But I had no idea then that he was going to use her as bait.

I had thought, as a matter of fact, that it was I who was going to have to use her, rather than the other way around. I had thought that I was going to have to land her to really sew things up tight with Marshall. But it wasn't working out that way at all. Marshall was pushing her at me and he was pushing hard. Maybe too hard.

Not that I didn't need all the assistance possible. Under normal circumstances I am regarded, among those who are privy to the facts, as something of a cocksman. I have been known to bed some of the best. Both for pleasure and for otherwise. But this Lisa. Well, Lisa was something special, that's all. She was in a league all of her own. Morley was really reaching when he asked me to get into her. Even with her daddy pushing.

Lisa. There was still a hint of her perfume. A little warning bell started clanging somewhere in the back of my head. I told myself I could really get to like that girl. I could get to like her a whole lot.

CHAPTER THREE

It is dusk by six o'clock of a February evening in Alamos. The sun has dropped down well behind the hills to the west. But there's still a pink glow along the jagged tops, a bright ribbon trimming the blue-black velvet jacket the hills put on at night, and it will stay there, on the lower ones at least, for about an hour. The cocktail hour.

I was a little late arriving at Marshall's Casa Alegre. The streets of the town are very narrow, hardly more than the width of a lane, and they are paved with cobblestone, which is always breaking up from the pressure of the heavy traffic it wasn't designed to withstand. That makes it slow going—especially in an old flatbed truck with the wide load my caravan presented.

I also had to park almost two blocks from the Casa Alegre. It looked as if every American in the town had been invited to Marshall's party and most of them had brought their cars. They jammed the streets approaching the house and the square in front of it. Cadillacs and Imperials, Buick and Ford station wagons, Jeeps and Broncos, Mustangs and Javelins, campers and pickup trucks.

The American colony in Alamos runs a considerable gamut. Some, like Marshall, are very rich, and they come down for perhaps only a month or so in the winter, particularly in January and February. They have the money for a variety of escapes. There are others, not quite so rich, who are more committed to their investment in their restored casas, and they may stay for a full six months, November through April. Together they account for the Cadillacs and Imperials.

Then there are the well-to-do. Retired business and professional men with a fair-sized wad stashed away and a pretty good pension to boot. Their casas are not quite so elaborate and they very definitely stay for the full six months. They can really stretch that old do-re-mi if they stay the whole winter in Alamos. Then, with the money they have saved, they can afford a nice trip in the summer, perhaps back home, or maybe even around the world on a freighter. They are more practical in their choice of cars. They drive the Buick and Ford station wagons, or, if they are sportsmen, the Jeeps and Broncos.

Next there is the artistic set. Artists, authors and others. They paint and write and indulge in their abnormalities. They come and go as their fortunes dictate. Most rent rather than own. The rich don't like their casas to stand vacant in their long absences. When a house is empty, things move in, such as rats and scorpions, spiders and bugs. So there is quite a trade in temporary accommodation. Palaces for rent. Three hundred bucks a month. Swimming pool and mozo thrown in. Available to artists, authors and others. People who appreciate a good thing and who drive Mustangs and Javelins.

Finally there are the hangers-on. Just enough coming in every month to be able to live in Mexico. Their casas are no hell, practically dumps, some of them, and the help comes only part time. They are very lucky if they can get away for a month or so at the height of the long hot summer. Their mode of transportation is extremely practical. Campers and pickup trucks. Some walk.

I was thinking about all these various types as I picked my way across the cobblestones to the Casa Alegre. There was one thing you had to say in favor of Marshall. He was democratic as hell. He was having them all to the party. A microcosm of elderly expatriate America. A dash of the artistic set. Spice with Lisa and Charlie Sparrow. Mix well.

It ought to be a real ball.

Marshall was working the door. He was wearing a tux, the thing he looked best in, and he had a yellow rose in his lapel, a reminder to all that while he had made his loot elsewhere his heart still belonged to Texas. He grabbed me with both hands. One shook. The other hugged.

"Hello, Charlie," he said. He said it right fondly.

I couldn't speak for a moment. Lisa was merely a flawless beauty when she had visited my caravan that morning. Tonight she was the queen of them all. The only word is exquisite. That's providing, of course, that a girl can be exquisite and sexy at the same time, because that's what she was. Exquisite and very, very sexy.

"Hi, date," she said.

" 'Lo," I managed. I got passed on to a beefy stranger. He was very dark, the Latin type, and rather handsome in his way, apart from a huge, remarkably hooked nose. Short-cropped graying hair. Thick black eyebrows. Cool blue eyes. Firm slash of mouth.

"I'd like you to meet my houseguest," Marshall said. "This is Mr. Ramon Velarde. A business associate and a very good friend." He paused for a moment. "This is the young man I've been telling you about," he informed Velarde. "My favorite author. Charlie Sparrow."

"Mr. Sparrow," Velarde said. We shook hands and he made a point of demonstrating his strong grip.

"My pleasure," I said. It wasn't particularly. He was almost crushing my hand.

Marshall escorted me a few steps down the hall. "You go get yourself a drink," he ordered. "We'll be finished up here in a little while. See you then."

" 'Bye, date," Lisa called. That sounded awfully final on her part.

I went in and joined the party.

The Casa Alegre, which, incidentally, means Happy House, is not especially lavish for Alamos. There are some real palaces hidden away behind the high walls that are linked together to form fortress blocks facing on the town's narrow streets. But then Marshall's month-a-year home wasn't exactly a dump either. It took up a full half block, the other half of which consisted of four ruins, none of them restored. The front of the house, facing the square, had a portal running the full length, supported by seven wide and graceful arches. There were six windows, very high and narrow, deep-set, barred. They were framed by the arches. Three on each side. The center arch displayed the entrance.

You passed through the front door and along a narrow hall directly to the open courtyard. The house was built all around the courtyard, just the one room deep, so that they all had a through breeze, which amounted to a must in the summer. There was also a portal that went all around the courtyard. Despite the large swimming pool at the far end, the stands of stately palms, the profusion of flowers and shrubs, the courtyard and its surrounding portals could handle two hundred guests easily. It was doing that now.

There was a choice of four bars. I picked the closest and started threading my way to it. I said hello, how are you, nice day, isn't it, what's new with you, you old bastard, you, and assorted other greetings to a variety of slight acquaintances but didn't stop for any more than that. They all had drinks. I find it very difficult to converse with anyone who has a drink when my hot little paw is empty. It's psychological. I hope.

The bartender was new. I had never seen him before, not here, or at any of the other homes, and I had been a not infrequent guest about town since my arrival. This normally wouldn't have bothered me. Bartenders come and bartenders go. But there were two things wrong with this fellow. One, he didn't know what the hell he was doing, and, two, he wasn't a Mexican. He was more like an Italian. In Alamos, when you hire a bartender, you hire a Mexican. Not an Italian. That is a very firm rule.

"A martini," I said. "If you make it strong enough, I won't bother you the rest of the night, okay?"

He grinned at me. He had two teeth missing. "Which is it?" he asked. "You want a double? A triple? A home run?"

"A home run," I said. I took a better look at him. He had a lot of scar tissue. It was really piled up over his eyes. Some of it was of fairly recent vintage. Perhaps this was why he hadn't bothered to replace those two teeth. They were only going to get knocked out again.

H. H. Goding joined me. That was okay on my part. I happened to like him a whole lot. He was one of the hangers-on in Alamos. One of the very first Americans to "discover" the town. He had arrived twenty years before, a gold watch, the one presented at his retirement, his only possession of any note, plus the five thousand dollars he had sewed into his hip pocket. He had bought himself a small ruin, which you could get for that price in those days, and he had gradually fixed it up over the years, pinching a few bucks a month from his social security. He had himself a pretty nice casa now. He lived in it year-round. Every six months he hitched a ride to the border to renew his turista permit. Then straight back to Alamos.

"How's by you?" H. H. Goding asked.

"Fine," I said. "And you?"

"Fantastic," he said.

H. H. Goding's favorite word was fantastic. He was eighty-five, and this tired old world, as far as he was concerned, was still fantastic. I had known him for just the two weeks. I regretted all the years that had gone before.

The bartender handed me my martini. When he said a home run, what he meant was, he meant out of the ball park. H. H. Goding regarded the size of it with open admiration.

"Fantastic," he said. He tried to steal it but I foiled him.

I eased him away from the bar and we talked about hunting for a while. I told him about the buck I had spooked. He predicted that it would be back in a couple of days. It had been a dry winter, with much less rain than normal, and water holes were hard to come by, he said. Finally I introduced the subject of the bartender.

"You ever see him work bar before?" I asked.

"No."

"Does he live in town?"

"No."

"You're sure about that?"

"Yes."

He asked me why the interest. I said I was thinking of becoming a friend of the family. He gave me that wise old look of his and we talked about broads.

He said I should be making it with Maggie. I told him I was saving myself for Lisa. He said I was a great guy. Tall, dark and handsome. Intelligent, dashing and debonair. Talented, humorous and well-mannered. A boon companion, a skilled raconteur, a fabulous cocksman. He said I was one hell of a guy, fantastic if you please, and he really meant *fantastic,* but he was of the considered opinion I was saving something I wouldn't be able to spend. Not with Lisa.

"You sure know how to hurt a guy," I said.

"You ain't been hurt," H. H. Goding said. "Yet."

We parted on that note. I told him I had forgotten my Viceroys. He said I also had forgotten my limitations. I worked my way over to one of the stands of palms. I sat down on the brick encasement, put my drink beside me, lit a cigarette and—moving my hand back for the drink—knocked it off the ledge. It fell in the dirt at the base of a palm. I took out my handkerchief to pick it up. That palm was going to have a hangover tomorrow morning.

Maggie came by a few moments later. "Mr. Wonderful," she began.

"Lady Desperate," I countered.

That hurt her. The big hazel eyes blinked. "That wasn't very kind."

I made the obvious reply and the conversation quickly disintegrated into an exchange of clichés.

"Let's not fight."

"You just got yourself a truce."

"That's not exactly a victory."

"You can't win them all."

"Neither can you."

The opinion seemed to be unanimous. Besides Marshall, there were only three people in town who knew me even slightly well, H. H. Goding, Maggie and Tyler. Now I had heard from all three regarding my chances with Lisa. Tyler had expressed his opinion that morning. He figured she was his. Not mine.

It wasn't a topic I particularly wanted to pursue with Maggie. To change the subject, I asked her if she wanted another drink. She said that she did indeed, and we went to get it together. I was careful to take her to other than an Italian bar.

"I meant what I said this morning," Maggie told me after we'd got our drinks.

"About leaving soon?"

She nodded.

"When?"

"The end of March. I've got to give a month's notice on the house."

"Where will you go?"

She stared down into her scotch. "I'm not sure. Not back home. Too many memories there."

I wondered about what kind of memories. While she had pumped me, I really didn't know too much about Maggie Hilton. I knew she was a divorcée, I knew no children were involved, I knew she was fairly well fixed—as a result of the divorce, or in her own right, was not clear—and I knew back home was Seattle. I also knew she looked a little bit like the young Lana Turner.

"It's a big country," I said.

"Isn't it?"

"Cheer up, for God's sake. You'll manage."

"Will I?"

Maggie moved on shortly afterward. We had a truce. An uneasy truce. I'd also been given a deadline. The end of March. I sipped at my martini. It was a single—a very safe, on-base single. A lot can happen between the middle of February and the end of March.

I got involved in the usual cocktail conversation with a variety of townspeople. There were two main topics. Their problems with the Mexican help. How exciting it was to be the guest of a man who might at any moment formally announce that he was a candidate for the presidency of the United States.

"He'd be crazy to do it," a little old lady told me.

"Why?"

"You listen to the radio, don't you?"

"I even read the papers."

"You heard they tried for the governor of Maine?"

That was last week.

"That was last week," I said. "Who's they?"

"It's a conspiracy," the little old lady said. She looked around apprehensively. "I wouldn't be surprised if there was an assassin right here at this party."

"You don't say?" I said. I wouldn't have been surprised either. Not in the least.

Ace King cornered me. "How about it?"

"About what?"

"The dam. Dutch and me are going in the morning. We're taking off at five."

I shook my head. "No. I've got the book."

"Why don't you write at night?"

"I can't," I told him. "I can only write when the sun shines. It does something for my batteries."

"Okay," Ace said. "The next time it rains, I'm coming over to get you, and we're going fishing, hear?"

"The next time it rains," I agreed.

He went away happy.

"Quite a crowd, isn't it?" David Snell said.

"Quite," I admitted.

His soft brown eyes moved over me. David was an artist and a good one. His stuff was hanging all over the town. He had a couple on the living room walls of the Casa Alegre. One of the church, the other of a kid and burro, the kid leading it, the burro loaded down with firewood. He also did portraits. He wanted to do mine.

"I wish you would," he said.

"Would what?"

He smiled limply. "You know. Sit."

"I've told you. I can't spare the time."

"I could come out to your caravan. Paint while you worked."

"That would bother me," I told him. It really would.

He went away unhappy. You win some, you lose some.

Lisa claimed me about a half-hour later. By that time I was working on my third martini. It would have to be the last for the evening. Four and I'm inclined to get a bit lippy.

"Date," Lisa said. She hooked an arm in mine. "How is it going? Enjoying yourself?"

"I am now," I said.

She smiled up at me and the pressure of her arm increased. "Let's go somewhere so we can talk."

"I know a great little motel in Oregon," I said.

She laughed. "We've got bedrooms right here."

She took me into the den, though. It was on the west side of the house. The quiet side because the ruins in the block were to the west. Like the other rooms, the den was elegant in its simplicity, which is hard to carry off. The Spanish have a special knack for it. One of their kinder legacies to Mexico.

The ceiling was at least twenty feet high. The beams, rough poles, a wood resistant to termites, were placed very close together, a tight column of supports for the sixteen-inch bricks that formed the roof. The walls were made of the same bricks, covered with a smooth plaster, painted an off-white. There was an oval brick fireplace in one corner. The windows were high and narrow in deep casements, thin bars on the outside, wooden shutters on the inside. The floor was a glistening sheet of marble tiles. Standard construction for the restored casas of Alamos.

Lisa settled in an overstuffed chair beside the fireplace. It had a small fire going and the flames did nice things to her hair. She took a sip of her drink. "I want to know all about you," she said.

"I thought your daddy told all?"

She wrinkled the chiseled nose. "Not really. Just the stuffy part. What a great writer you are. The places you've been. The assignments you've had."

"Does daddy check like that very often?"

"Check?"

"Check," I repeated. "Investigate. I haven't been giving him any details. He got that on his own—or rather he had somebody get it for him."

"Really?"

"Really."

She took another sip of her drink and put it aside. "That's something new," she said. "He's never done that before." She smiled prettily. "What do you think it all means?"

I took out my Viceroys. She accepted one and I lit it for her. "I was thinking of asking him that."

"Don't," she said.

"Why not?"

She waved away the smoke. "It would spoil it."

"Spoil what?"

"The fun, silly. The fun of guessing. What's your guess?"

Her file said she was twenty. She didn't look that old at the moment. More like sixteen. An exquisite and very sexy sixteen. "This is going to sound a little presumptuous," I said.

"You look the type."

"I had the idea he was going to offer me a job," I told her. "If he goes after the presidency, he's going to need writers, a lot of them. I'm a writer."

"Would you accept a job?"

"I'm not sure."

"Why not?"

"I'm not sure about that either."

She studied her cigarette. "You're not afraid, are you?"

"You mean the physical danger?"

"Yes," she said. "It's not a very healthy occupation, is it? Wanting to be President, I mean. If you were closely associated with a man like that—well, you just might get in the way of a bullet, mightn't you?"

"That had crossed my mind."

She studied me for a moment. "How many is it now?" Surely she knew. Even the little old lady knew the score. "Four dead," I said. "Two seriously wounded. One close call."

She grimaced.

"You think he'll take the chance?"

The subject obviously didn't appeal to her. She drank her drink and smoked her smoke. "That was one guess. Care to try for two?"

"It's your turn."

"This is going to sound a little presumptuous," she said.

I laughed. She was pretty quick. Exquisite, very sexy, and quick.

"You know how old I am?"

It was an excuse to examine her. I took my sweet time about it. She was very definitely too good to be true. "Twenty-two. Maybe twenty-three."

"Twenty," she said.

"You look older."

"You're a liar."

"I am. You look sixteen."

"A very bad liar."

I shrugged helplessly and nursed my martini.

"It's time I was married," she said.

"You shouldn't have any trouble doing that."

"Now, that is the truth," she grinned. She showed me her profile. "Did you ever see a more gorgeous hunk of woman?"

"Never."

She turned back to face me. She sat up and pulled back her shoulders. Her breasts almost popped out of her dress. "Radiating quite so much raw sex appeal?"

"Never."

She held up her left hand. There was a ruby on her ring finger. I had noticed that at the front door. It would choke a pelican. "With a richer daddy?"

"Never."

"That's my guess," she said. "Father met you, he liked you, he checked you out. You came up smelling roses." The green eyes were flat again. "I've never done that well on my own. Father never was very fond of my choices. When he checked—well, let's just say those weren't no roses, Charlie."

"I thought you said this was his first check?"

"I did. So I'm a liar. A very bad liar."

I finished my martini regretfully. The third single. Safe every time.

"That's my guess," she repeated.

"A little presumptuous on daddy's part," I said.

She didn't laugh. Neither did I. We had worn out that one.

"He dragged me down here," she said. "It was all so terribly obvious. I felt like a fish on a platter."

I didn't say anything.

"You want the fish?" she asked softly.

"I can't have," I said.

She stabbed out her cigarette. "How observant of you..."

Sure. We were both quick. Sheet lightning. Falling stars. Toad's tongues.

"I'm glad we had our talk," she said. She started to get up. End of talk.

I was trying to think of something fitting, self-immolation, perhaps, when the sound of voices, raised in anger, came from the adjoining room. Lisa swung her head around. One of the voices was Marshall's. The other's was also a male. They were having an argument. A bitter one.

All I could catch were the swear words. "Who's that with him?" I asked.

"Shhh!" Lisa said. She didn't seem worried. Just interested.

The door of the adjoining room was flung open. Ramon Velarde came striding out. He was mad as hell and he passed between us as if we didn't exist.

"How are you two getting along?"

I looked back to the open door. Marshall was standing there, very cool, very relaxed. His grin was casual and honest.

"We were just saying how much we like each other," I said.

I didn't get a chance until after dinner. It was served buffet style, of course, and all the portals were crowded, because that's where most of the chairs were situated. Lisa had sat with me for only a few bites. Then she was off, making the rounds, playing the hostess.

The guest bedrooms were located along the north wall. There were four of them, all identical, all with private bath. The second one I tried was Velarde's. He was the only guest who wore double-breasted suits. Actually, he was the only guest, because the three other rooms were occupied by Marshall's staff, a special assistant, an accountant and a woman secretary. I had files on all three of them. They had been with him forever. Velarde was something else. A new face. An unknown.

The double-breasted suits, their labels said, were made in Mexico City, all by the same tailor. Francisco. I rubbed one of the sleeves between my fingers. Expensive. Marshall, Lisa, Velarde. All so damn expensive.

The closet produced nothing. I tried the bureau. There was a Luger under the silk shirts in the top drawer. The clip was full and there also was a shell in the chamber. One extra shot.

That was all. No cards, no papers, no documents. No membership in SMERSH. No floor plan for the basement of the White House.

I went into the bathroom. No news there either. Except that Velarde had false teeth. And that was merely an assumption on my part. He might use the stickum to stickum something else.

There was a thumbprint on the cabinet mirror. I dusted it, lifted it and put the tab in my shirt pocket. Five will get you ten it was going to belong to the chambermaid.

There was a figure standing in the shadows when I slipped back onto the portal.

"What the hell do you think you're doing?" Tyler asked.

"Stealing stuff," I said. "Money, jewels, silverware. You want to split it?"

"Up yours," he said.

It's a wonderful world. We all love each other. We all love each other very much.

CHAPTER FOUR

The plane came over shortly after ten o'clock the next morning. It made a low pass and kept on going. I got outside and caught enough of it for positive identification. A Skycraft Turbo Baron. I changed my shirt, unhooked the caravan, and drove into town.

There was nothing doing when I got to the airport. The plane was tied down and the airport manager was already asleep on his cot under the wing. That's the kind of job I'd like. On a bed in the shade.

I stopped at the roadside for a minute to admire the Baron. The world's fastest light twin. It cruises at 320 mph. Has a range of almost 1,500 miles. Takes a ton load above 30,000 feet.

The glistening red baby sitting in front of me had complete VHF Nav/Com system and ADF. Full IFR capability with dual avionics, radar and de-icing equipment. I had flown her a few times. But not over Mount Whitney on one engine.

I honked the horn and awakened the airport manager. Then I drove on into town and parked in the business plaza. I bought some vegetables in the market, picked up a pair of sandals in the leather shop, and stopped for a beer in the tavern across the street.

Hobart was sitting at a table in a corner. He had four cans of beer in front of him. Two were already empty.

"Join me," Hobart said.

He hadn't changed much. A big man, the lifeguard type, with a huge head, bull neck, barrel chest. He was in his late fifties and his hair was so sparse that he had taken to shaving his skull. He had lots everywhere else, though. Big, bushy black eyebrows, a thick black mustache, a matting on the backs of his hands, at the base of his neck, protruding from his ears, poking out of his nostrils. An ape with a bald and glistening skull. The last time I had seen him, which had been almost a year before, he had been wearing a red wool shirt and a dirty brown suede jacket. He was still wearing them.

Hobart took a piece of chalk and two beans out of his jacket pocket. He drew a circle on the tabletop with the chalk and placed the two beans in the center.

"This one is mine," Hobart said.

I nodded.

We sat watching the beans. Presently his started to jump. It went hippity-hippity-hop out of the circle.

"You buy," Hobart said.

I examined my bean. I shook it up and bounced it. I listened carefully to its insides. It was a very sickly bean and it wouldn't jump if you goosed it.

"The luck of the draw," Hobart said. He picked up his third beer. I reached for the fourth and he grabbed it away indignantly. "You also buy your own."

I signaled for one more beer.

Hobart apologized for me to the waiter. He explained that I was a cheap, stupid, perverse, pig-fornicating gringo. He said only a real tight asshole like myself would be so mean as to buy only one beer at a time. He said it was a wonder they allowed me in the joint.

"You just passing through?" I asked hopefully.

"Unfortunately," he said. "I hear they've got a great whore-house down the road a piece." He wiped his chin. "Get it? Down the road—a piece ..."

"Unfortunately," I said.

Hobart looked me over while he polished off his third beer. He seemed immensely satisfied with my appearance but he didn't say so. "You look lousy, kid," he said. "You must be working too hard. Late nights?"

"Yeah," I said. "You know how it is with us writer fellows. Pounding a typewriter round the clock."

He smiled knowingly.

I took my voice scrambler out of my pocket and put it in the middle of the table. It's a fairly small gadget about the size of a traveling alarm clock. When it is turned on, they can aim all the electronic snooping gear in the world at you, and all they'll hear is a bunch of static, like the Voice of America in Estonia.

"How are things out at the ranch, kid?" Hobart asked.

"Fine," I told him. "It's a regular little trailer court. I'm parked near a well and hooked into both water and power. It's almost like home."

He smiled again. "I thought you'd like it."

"It's okay," I said. I hadn't been aware that he made the arrangements.

Hobart reached into his jacket pocket and took out a wallet. He passed it to me. "I've got some great new pictures of the kids."

I took it. They were great pictures. They were also great kids. But the last picture wasn't of his brood. It was a very flattering photograph of Maggie Hilton.

"What do you think of the last one?" Hobart asked.

"She's the prettiest one of the lot."

"You like her, huh?"

"She's okay."

"You haven't been telling her any state secrets?"

"Hardly ...."

"That's good," Hobart said. "She's a strange one. You've got to watch her."

"Spoiled?"

"That," Hobart said. "And a fibber. You can't believe a word she says."

He took back the wallet. He didn't say anything else about his wayward child. That meant he didn't know anything else. Which was great. Just great.

"How's the book coming?" Hobart asked.

"Along," I told him. "I'm just finishing chapter twelve. The king likes the white knight very much. He's thinking of taking him into his court. But the princess couldn't care less."

"I could see that coming," Hobart said. "What's next? The white knight keeps trying?"

"Sure. You can't count him out yet. I don't think he'll make it, though. This princess. Wow ..."

"But the king still takes him into his court?"

"That's hard to say. The princess and the court bit seem to go together somehow. It's almost as if the king wanted the white knight to have both or nothing. A very complicated plot."

Hobart frowned. "Try not to make it too complicated."

"I'm trying," I said. "But these ideas keep coming to me. I'm thinking of introducing a black knight. He's a guest at the palace, a long-time business associate, a close friend, the king says. A tough-looking hombre who wears double-breasted armor and hails from the capital to the south. He and the king cross verbal swords and later the white knight finds a loaded lance in this hombre's bedroom."

Hobart went a little white at the corners of his mouth.

"You want to help me on some character development?" I asked.

"Why not?" he said. "You know how I like to help."

I gave him the tab with the thumbprint. "That's him. Or maybe the chambermaid."

"I don't like the maybe part."

"It's the best I can do."

Hobart put the tab in his wallet. He was frowning again when he shoved it into his jacket pocket. Somewhere along the line he had lost his sense of humor.

"There's one other thing," I said.

The frown deepened.

I gave him a hankerchief-wrapped glass that once contained a home run. "This is from a fine Italian hand. It also needs character development."

"Have you got a start?" Hobart asked tiredly.

"He's a big bully. He stole a job from a Mexican bartender. Right under the king's nose."

"Jesus," Hobart said. He stood up. He hadn't even finished his fourth beer. That was very unlike Hobart.

"One more thing," I said.

He stared down at me suspiciously.

"If somebody wanted to bump off the king, he could do it real easy," I said. "The white knight could have done it yesterday morning. He was on a butte and the king came riding up and— well, if the damn thing was loaded, no more king, that's all."

Hobart fidgeted with the back of his chair. "He hasn't announced..."

"No," I admitted. "But it's general knowledge that he's considering it. It was the talk of the ball."

He didn't answer.

"We need a palace guard," I said.

Hobart thought for a moment. "No, kid," he said. "It's not the pattern. They never get hit until they announce."

It occurred to me that patterns can and do change. "I can't be responsible..."

Hobart smiled. "Oh, but you are, kid," he said. "You are."

I spent the afternoon hunting doves on the ranch with Marshall and Velarde. We had made the arrangements the night before, as I was leaving the party, but it had been for just the two of us, myself and Marshall. There had been no mention then of him bringing along Velarde. When they showed up together, I was afraid I was in for a bum afternoon, but they were the best of friends again, neither showing any signs of the heated argument of the previous evening.

We circled back to the base of the hills at the north end of the ranch and then split up to work our way back south. I took the center, Marshall on the east, Velarde on the west. We agreed to shoot only white-wings. They are half as big again as the solid grays. I frankly can't see shooting any kind of doves. Even the white-wings are good for only two mouthfuls. But I could hardly pass up this opportunity to spend the afternoon with Marshall.

The pickings were easy. The ranch owner, a Chicago businessman, hadn't been down since the spring, and the land hadn't been shot all winter except for the two bucks I had taken at my water hole in the arroyo. Lulled into a false sense of security, heavy from gorging on sesame seed, the white-wings wouldn't flush until you were almost on top of them, and then they would light as soon as they got over the first rise. The way the three of us were spread out, working in a line down the half-mile width of the ranch, it was a slaughter, actually. We could pick them off both coming and going, when they flushed, and as they settled again.

I had my limit in less than an hour. The others apparently hadn't done as well. Velarde, on my right, was still blasting away like gangbusters, and there was an occasional shot on my left from Marshall. I kept moving along with them, flushing the doves to either side, but not shooting.

We had arranged to meet at the big water hole at the south end of the ranch. I got there first and plopped down in the shade of a mesquite. There was nothing else to do, so I started cleaning my birds, wrapping them in little individual poly bags. They really were all feathers and guts. The carcasses were smaller than squabs.

Marshall showed up about five minutes later. He looked tired but happy and his game bag was bulging.

"How did it go?" I asked.

"Twelve," he grinned. "You?"

"I got my limit."

He eased himself onto a flat rock. "I should have easy," he said. "It was like a shooting gallery. But I'm a bit rusty, I guess, and I haven't got the eye I used to have, that's for damn sure."

"You used to hunt a lot?"

He shook his head. "Not really. Too busy getting rich. But I got out once in a while."

A clatter of gunfire echoed along the slopes to the west of us. Three shots fired in rapid succession. It takes an exceptional shot to get three away in one flush. Or else Velarde didn't know what the hell he was doing.

"Your friend is eager," I said.

"Sounds like it," Marshall agreed. His mind seemed elsewhere.

I had been too busy shooting to keep track but the thought struck me that there had been an awful lot of gunfire on the west as we worked down the ranch. Velarde must have used up almost two boxes of shells by now. That was a bit much in a shooting gallery with a limit of fifteen.

"You always do that?" Marshall asked. He was watching me pulling feathers.

"No," I said. "I just thought it would be a good idea. I don't want to have a mess around the caravan."

He smiled. "You do keep it clean."

"Yes," I said. "I like it that way."

"I always thought hippies were sort of dirty."

"I'm not a hippie."

He smiled again. "I know."

"I know you know," I told him.

He sat there for a while watching me. The doves cleaned easily. The feathers practically fell out. The only tough part was the leading edge of the wings. And I had the guts down to a science.

"You're not hitting it off too well with Lisa?" he asked.

It was my turn to smile. "No."

"Do you like her?"

"She's a very beautiful woman."

"I didn't ask you that."

"Yes," I said slowly. "I like her. I think I could learn to like her very much."

He took his time unwrapping a long narrow cigar. He didn't offer me one. When he got it going, he asked, "What's the problem?"

"No problem," I said. "I'm just not her kind of a guy. That's hardly a problem."

He blew out a stream of smoke. I had seen somebody else do that recently. Lisa. "It is for me," he said.

"Oh?" I was going to say more but decided to let him do the talking.

"I was hoping..." He stopped, plainly flustered. "Well, to be quite frank about it, I was hoping you two might really click."

"That was obvious," I said. "To me and to Lisa. She complained last night that you dragged her down here. A fish on a platter, she said, and if we're being frank about it, I really can't blame her for being angry. Or standoffish."

Marshall examined his cigar critically. "I was afraid of that happening. But I really had no other choice. You were here and she was there. You were busy writing your book. I couldn't move you...."

"Excuse me," I said. "I don't wish to be impolite, Mr. Marshall, but I think I have the right, all things considered, to ask you a rather rude question."

"Go ahead."

"Two questions. Why are you in such a hurry to marry off your daughter? And why pick on me as bridegroom material?"

There was the sound of two more shots from the west. Well spaced this time. Too far apart to make sense.

Marshall waited until the echoes died away. "I'll be going back home in a week or so," he said. "I've made up my mind. When I get back, I'm going to formally announce my candidacy, start preparing for the primaries."

"You are?" The sounds of gunfire were so recent the two of them went together. His announcement. Shots. "That's a dangerous step to take—these days."

"I know," he said. "It's been a difficult decision. I've been under a considerable amount of pressure not to run." He managed a tight smile. "There has been pressure, naturally, from the other side, too. *Somebody* has to run for President."

I sat staring at him. There was no arguing with that part of it.

"If I run," he said, flicking his ash thoughtfully, "I'm going to run to win, not for the fun of it. I'm going to pull out all the stops. I'm not going to let anybody or anything stand in my way."

"Such as Lisa?"

"That's right," he said. "Lisa, as you know, is a very headstrong, very attractive girl. It's not..." He was again flustered. "Let's say I don't relish the idea of her running around single while I'm campaigning for the presidency. She could get into a lot of trouble between now and November. I'd prefer her married. Or at least engaged."

"Settled down?"

"Exactly."

"And that's your problem?"

"One of my problems."

I felt kind of sorry for him then. For him, for Lisa, for Charlie Sparrow. "That answers one question," I said. "Now, how about the other one? Why me?"

"Lisa was engaged once," Marshall answered carefully. "Two years ago. She was eighteen then, in her third year of college, and the boy was twenty-four, a captain in the infantry. She had her education to finish and he had a war that wasn't quite over. I asked them to wait."

"And they did?"

"Yes." He paused and considered. "I think that was the last time she ever abided by my wishes in something of major importance."

"I gather he didn't come back?"

"I'm afraid not," Marshall said. He looked at me over his cigar. "If the boy had lived—if he was sitting here right now—there would be two of you characters. You look like him in so many ways...."

"Oh?"

"It's more than that," Marshall said. "Not just in appearance. There are a lot of little things. The same presence. The same style. You know what I mean?"

The best laid plans, I thought. That was something I hadn't known. That was something that had been missed by Morley. Oh, you're so God damn smart, Morley. You're positively brilliant. But you really screwed up this time. "You better find yourself another boy," I told Marshall.

"You're not interested?"

"I'm interested," I said. "Christ, I'm only human, you know. But you're going about it all the wrong way. You don't mend a girl's broken heart by showing her a ghost. It's wrong. All wrong."

Marshall took a last pull on his cigar. He tossed it aside carelessly. "Perhaps you are right."

I was, I thought, but I should have kept silent, not said anything. It didn't help matters for me to tell him that he had made a mistake. I could lose them both now. The girl *and* the job. The job was the important thing. If he ran, I was supposed to be right beside him, with him for every waking moment, guarding him all the way. He was my responsibility.

"No harm done, I hope," Marshall said. He stood up. "I apologize for involving you in this nonsense. It was just that…" He shrugged his broad shoulders. "Well, I guess I'm a dreamer at times, that's all. I saw it as a way to make everybody happy. Yourself included."

"I would have been very happy," I told him.

Velarde had approached without either of us hearing him. He announced his presence by tossing his game bag on the ground in front of me. It was a large bag and it was bulging with doves. There must have been at least two dozen in it. He had more in the pockets of his jacket. He started pulling them out and tossing them on the ground. He hadn't restricted his shooting to white-wings. He had taken a lot of the little grays.

I picked one of them up. Its head had been crushed flat. The others were the same. I thought of a couple of ways the heads could have been squashed like that. Between two rocks. Or between the thumb and forefinger of a man with extremely powerful hands. "You're over your limit," I said.

Velarde smiled down at me. "What does it matter? There are so many of them. And who is to know?"

That evening I didn't move out of the caravan. There was nothing doing of note in the town. Most everybody was resting up after Marshall's bash. I ate a dove dinner, had a couple of beers, listened to records for a while, and then reread the two reports brought down by Hobart.

One was a completely new file. It was on Maggie Hilton. Real name: Doris Dubois. An interesting name. There once was a French cardinal named Dubois. Guillaume Dubois, 1656–1723, chief adviser to the regent, Philippe d'Orléans. Astute diplomat. I tried to think of some others. There was a Guy Pène du Bois. The American painter and art critic. There was a William Edward

Burghardt Du Bois. He was an American, too. A Negro. An author and the editor of *Crisis*. There's a city called Du Bois in central Pennsylvania. Settled in 1812. Railroad shops, coal mining, metal and textile plants ...

Dubois, huh? She didn't look French. She looked a little bit like the younger Lana Turner. Age: 32. Birthplace: Seattle, Washington. Parents: both dead. Other next of kin: unknown. Marital status: single, but that was just a guess, *as far as can be determined*, the file said. The story of the recent divorce, at any rate, was a lot of crap, because there wasn't any record of it. Occupation: unemployed. Last previous position as a translator with the Research Division, Hughes Aircraft Laboratories, Laguna Beach, California. Reason for termination: employee left of own volition. Date of termination: February 10, 1971. Whereabouts since: unknown. Until, of course, she had turned up in Alamos, Sonora, Mexico, very hot to trot for Charlie Sparrow.

I lifted the pages of my calendar and checked the previous year. February 10, 1971, was a Wednesday, and so that added one more unanswered question to the file. Why did Doris Dubois, alias Maggie Hilton, quit her job, of her own volition, in the middle of the week? The file should have explained that. You don't voluntarily quit a job on a Wednesday. You quit on a Friday. The end of a pay period. The file should have explained that. It was a lousy file. I tossed it aside.

The other was an updating on Lisa Marshall. Real name: Lisa Marshall. Now that was a switch, wasn't it? The new part was in answer to a number of questions I had fired off to Morley as soon as Marshall told me he was trying to get Lisa to come down to Alamos. I wanted to know what kind of a girl she was, *really*, and now that I had the results of a solid week of deep probing—well, I was glad I had asked, but sorry, too.

Lisa Marshall had been around the block a few times in the two years since her dashing young captain had got zapped in

Viet Nam. There was a lot of stuff about the captain. He was a nice guy, bright, ambitious, promising. It had him taped from A to Z. Only one thing was missing. The fact that he looked like me.

I couldn't figure it. Even before my request for a hard dig, when they were just making a routine investigation, surely someone would have checked out the captain, gone over some yearbooks, seen some photographs of him. The thing couldn't have been handled that carelessly.

Or was it carelessness?

Perhaps it was the other way around. Perhaps Morley had seen the likeness. Perhaps that was why he had chosen me and not one of any number of others for the job. That made more sense than the idea that somebody had done a really shoddy check on the captain. Up until now, I reminded myself, I had been one of Morley's amateurs, not a pro. Previous assignments had been in connection with my regular magazine work. So *Look* is sending you to Spain? And you're going to be talking to Franco and members of his Cabinet? Well, when you are doing that, Charlie, would you mind very much ... ?

It had been that way all the previous times. The magazine writer with the sideline. This was the first time I had ever quit my job and gone the whole route for Morley. And why had he wanted me so badly? Why had he been so persuasive? Oh, sure, you are a cocksman, Charlie. But let's face it. Not that hot. You are not the idol of millions. This job requires that you have something more going for you—such as a certain likeness to a certain captain.

But if so, why hadn't Morley told me, for Christ's sake? Why not prepare me for that shocked look on Lisa's face when she rode up and first saw Charlie Sparrow?

Why? Because there was no reason why I should know, why I should be prepared, that's why. Had I known, my reaction to her shock might have been wrong, and if it was wrong, it could have been noticed. By Marshall. Or Lisa. That's why.

But it still didn't make sense. It was a weird pitch, a real curve ball, I thought again. I told myself that you don't mend a girl's broken heart by showing her a ghost. That is not the way to go about it.

Or is it? Morley thought so, and so, obviously, did Marshall. Morley and Marshall thought alike. Two against one. And you still couldn't count out the white knight. Perhaps, when the shock wore off, when she got used to the idea, the princess might change her mind.

I returned my attention to the updated file. If Morley had held out on me on one thing, he could have held out on a lot of other stuff, too. He could have had the whole story right from the start and decided not to give it to me until I was ready for it. And when was I ready? When I asked, that's when, and after—very definitely *after*—I had my first meeting with Lisa. That would explain why Hobart was late making contact. Why he hadn't shown up until the morning after the party at the Casa Alegre.

The information in the updated file was pretty rough. It wasn't the kind of things you told a man about a lady and then told that same man he would fall in love with her the moment he saw her. Even if she was as beautiful as Lisa.

The way to handle it was to let him see her first. Let him have that first moment in all its dazzling glory. Let him see only the nice part. How exquisite. How very, very sexy. How quick. Let the poor bastard have his love at first sight. *Then* tell him.

Tell him that after the dashing young captain got zapped the princess was very broken up. Tell him that after a period of deep despondency she emerged as a different kind of a girl. Tell him she simply couldn't care less about a lot of things. Whisper in the white knight's ear and give him the word that the princess is a dirty whore.

I got up off the bed and put both files in the safe. It was almost ten o'clock. There was a Voice of America news broadcast then from Washington. I turned on the radio and waited.

The first item disclosed that Senator James Burney, chairman of the Senate Insular Affairs Committee, leading figure in the Republican Party, recently announced candidate for the presidency of the United States, had been killed in the crash of a light plane near Delano, California. He and three others aboard had died instantly when the aircraft crashed and exploded in a grapefruit orchard. The cause of the crash had not been determined. Sabotage was suspected.

The others killed were Burney's administrative assistant, his secretary and a young advertising executive who had only recently joined his staff. I knew the latter slightly. He had been given the same word as me. You are responsible.

Oh, you're so God damn smart, Morley. You are positively brilliant. But are you smart enough this time?

CHAPTER FIVE

There were no riders the next morning. The big pot of coffee waiting on the stove went untouched. The two dozen fresh pages of manuscript sitting by the typewriter went unread. The game, it seemed, was over, and my side hadn't scored. It had come close—but it hadn't made the board.

Around ten o'clock I unhooked the caravan and drove the three miles into Alamos. For some reason, it had lost all its appeal for me, and all I could see as I cruised the narrow streets was a dirty, foul-smelling, garbage-strewn, fly-blown town, and what they could do is, I thought, they could blacktop their Government Colonial Monument. They could blacktop it and then they could stuff it.

Lisa's Buick wasn't parked in front of the Casa Alegre. Nor, as far as I could determine, was it parked anywhere else in town, and so that meant she must have gone to Navojoa or perhaps Ciudad Obregón. Her third day and already she was bored.

Well, I've got news for you, Morley, I thought. I'm bored, too. Stiff. I parked the caravan in the business plaza and went into the tavern across from the leather shop. It was the only public place in town that smelled good to me. It fairly reeked of spilled beer.

The low brick building was really old, and while no one seemed to know the exact date it was erected, there was general agreement that it was one of the town's original buildings, which meant it went back to about the 1680's. So that's what it smelled of. Three centuries of spilled beer.

I went to the bar, got myself a small bottle of tequila, and took it to my usual corner. I wet the top of my glass with squeezed lime, piled the rim high with salt, and then filled it halfway up with the straight liquor. I finished that off very quickly and then made another and then settled down to watch the pool players.

One of them was very good. A skinny kid, not much more than fifteen, sixteen, and by the looks of him he had spent every one of those years indoors, bent over the green felt. He was more Spanish than Indian but he had the Indian's eye. I knew some pool halls where he could make a fortune. Here, however, he was playing for beer, not money. Beer and the joy of the game.

He was very good and I watched him for a long time. No matter what the man is doing, playing pool, making pizza, or digging a grave, it is nice, I think, to watch a real professional in action. A man who really knows what he is doing. Who gets it right. Every time.

Unlike Charlie Sparrow.

I had put away almost half the bottle when she came in. She spotted me immediately and came swinging across to the table with that assured walk of hers. They ask the girls not to wear slacks in public in Mexico, but these were really a type of jodhpurs, not slacks, and besides, only an old fat ass would complain.

"Imagine," Lisa said. She sat down without being invited. She also helped herself to one of my Viceroys. I let her light it for herself, too.

"Good morning," I said finally.

"Isn't it?" she agreed brightly. "What have you got there? A drink or a salt lick?"

I stared at her tiredly. It was a lousy day and I wasn't up to trading smart talk with a whore. Even if she was without a doubt the prettiest one that had ever been brought to my attention.

"You going to buy me a drink?" she asked. She pulled off the silk scarf that was tied loosely around her hair. The soft mane of yellow gold fell to her throat.

"What kind?"

"Do they have bourbon?"

"It's terrible."

"Then buy me a terrible bourbon."

I ordered it for her and we sat looking at each other for a while, like two people who had a difficult, unattractive task awaiting them, and who were putting it off until the last possible moment.

"I'm afraid I was pretty much of a bitch the other night," Lisa said then.

I didn't compliment her on her wonderful grasp of the obvious. But then I didn't disagree with her, either.

"I mean it," she said. "I'm sorry for being a bitch and I apologize." The green eyes widened slightly. "Don't tell me it's already too late?"

I examined the label on my bottle. "No," I said. "It's just not necessary, that's all. Your father has explained your marked lack of enthusiasm for the Charlie Sparrow charm."

"Oh?"

"That's right," I said. "He told me of my resemblance..." I pushed the bottle aside and raised my glass. "Well, no apologies are necessary, that's all, and so let's just leave it at that, okay? I'll see you around and here's to a good and happy life."

She clicked her glass against mine, took a big sip of the bourbon, and made an elaborate face as it went down. *"Jesus."*

"I warned you."

"Please, sir," she said. "I came in to say I was sorry. Not to commit suicide." She made a show of depositing the glass at arm's length. "Listen, what say we get the hell out of this pool hall, Charlie?"

I eyed her doubtfully. "What have you got in mind?"

"A picnic," she said. "I've got a hamper full of goodies packed in the Buick. You interested?"

"Is there coffee in that hamper?"

"Lots of it."

"Then I'm interested," I told her.

We had the picnic at the base of the butte I had been perched on when Lisa had first come riding out to the ranch with Marshall. There was a little sandy bowl there amid the rocks in a stream bed meandering down out of the hills to join the arroyo. No matter how hot it got elsewhere, that little bowl, protected by large boulders and an umbrella of poplars, remained cool and verdant even at high noon. One other thing recommended it. Complete privacy.

"This *is* nice," Lisa breathed. She was stretched out on her back, her head propped up against a rock, gazing contentedly at the blue sky through a tangle of poplar branches.

"Thank you," I said. "It pleases me that you are pleased. Actually, you are quite privileged to be here, young lady. This is one of my very special and very private places. You are the first guest…"

She laughed huskily. "Special, huh? And just what is it that you do here that is so special?"

"Meditate," I said. "Here, I meditate…." I rolled over onto my side and pointed to the top of the butte. "There, I contemplate. We writer fellows spend a lot of time meditating and contemplating."

"You don't say?"

"I do say."

She was lost in thought for a while. "This book you are writing," she said then. "It's almost finished, isn't it? What are you going to do then?"

"If it sells, I'll write another, I suppose. If it doesn't, it's back to work…."

"Have you thought any more of working for my father?"

I raised my head to look at her. She was still staring up at the sky and it was impossible to tell whether she was sincerely interested in my future plans or was just making conversation. "He hasn't asked me," I pointed out.

"He may," she said. The words sounded almost like a warning.

I decided to let it go at that. She might know something, and if she did, I might still have a chance of working for Marshall, which was the object of the exercise. But rather than press it with her, I thought, I should just relax and wait to hear more from Marshall himself, and in the meantime do my best to take advantage of Lisa's sudden change of heart towards me—as evidenced by her apology and the fact that she had come looking for me with a picnic hamper.

"I'm having a rare day off," I said. "What say we forget the book and my dreary prospects of having to work for a living? Can't you think of a subject more in tune with this little corner of paradise? It took a great deal of effort on my part to lure you here and ..."

She laughed again. "Oh, God. You're not going to make a pass, are you, Charlie?"

"Why not?" I asked. I was watching her expression but my mind was on her updated file. She knew how to play the game and when the passes came spinning at her she never fumbled a damn one.

"Well," Lisa said. She sat up slowly with a look of determined sadness. "Picnic's over. Time to go home."

"All right," I said. "It's your picnic." I stood up and reached for her hands and pulled her to her feet. "You're sure about this ... ?"

"Yes," she said firmly.

That didn't make sense to me. It was too much out of character for her. I tightened my grip on her hands and pulled her to me. My intention had been to kiss her lightly on the cheek, but she was expecting a more direct approach, and she twisted her head away, banging her mouth against mine. That made it a very amateurish and unsatisfactory first kiss.

"That was sloppy," I said.

"Wasn't it?" she agreed. She seemed suddenly unsure of herself.

She had misjudged me, her eyes were saying, and my intended gentlemanly peck on her cheek, an appropriate way of rescuing both of us from a too stilted leave-taking, had been spoiled by her distrust.

"Now we must do it properly," I told her. I released her hands and moved mine up to cup the yellow hair. I held her head so that she could not twist away and I kissed her most properly. There was a moment's hesitation on her part and then the soft wet lips parted in warm response.

"Okay," I said, releasing her. "That was much better. *Now* we can go home...."

She looked at me wonderingly. If it was up to me, I thought, we wouldn't be going home, now would we? Not for a while yet at least.

"I think that's a very good idea."

Like hell she did. I had almost made up my mind to tell her so when a light twin's engines shattered the quiet of our private paradise. I couldn't see the plane through the dense cover of poplars but it passed so low over my caravan it could only mean one thing. The Red Baron was back.

Hobart was sitting at the same table. He seemed to have aged a lot recently. There were lines in his face that hadn't been apparent before. His eyes were dull, the sparkle all gone, and the lids were puffy, as if he hadn't had much sleep the past few nights. Even his skull had lost its glisten.

There were just the two beers in front of him. One was obviously for me. I sat down and took it.

"Bad news?" I asked.

"Very," Hobart said.

I took a sip of my beer. "I've got some good news. The book is coming along very well. The white knight and the princess are getting on much better."

He didn't seem particularly interested. "Oh?"

"They went on a picnic this afternoon," I said. "They had a nice time and it was sort of romantic. There's no telling what might have happened if the Red Baron hadn't showed up to spoil it all."

"Really?"

"Really," I said. "You may not believe this but it's true. The white knight kissed the princess and the princess kissed him back."

"That's nice," Hobart said. He hadn't touched his beer. The level was right up to the zip-top opening.

"What's wrong?"

"Everything," Hobart said. "You remember asking my help in character development?"

I nodded.

Hobart fiddled nervously with the voice scrambler. It was very unusual for him to do that. He thought the scrambler was a lot of crap. Normally.

"Here's how it turned out," Hobart said. He unzipped the inner pocket of his suede jacket and passed me a small manila envelope. "It's in there. You have to read between the lines. After you digest it, you're supposed to eat it, and that's quite an order."

"The double-breasted loaded lance?"

Hobart shook his head. "No. He checks out fine. He is what he says he is. A business associate and a good friend."

"The fine Italian hand?"

"He's okay, too," Hobart said. "He's one of the king's most trusted bodyguards. He made quite a record for himself years ago but that's all in the past. He's a straight man now."

I tapped my teeth. "The missing choppers?"

"He boxes to keep in shape."

That left Maggie. "The French lady?"

"Nothing new from my end," Hobart said. "Sorry about that. You'll just have to play it by ear."

I was confused at this point. I fingered the manila envelope.

"Put it away," Hobart ordered.

I did.

Hobart sat staring at me. He didn't bring out any beans, he didn't talk dirty, and he didn't drink his beer.

"I am confused at this point," I said.

"We are all confused," Hobart said. "We are confused at the highest levels of the land. And all because the white knight got sloppy."

"Sloppy?"

Hobart made a motion toward my pocket containing the manila envelope. "It's in there. When you read it, which will be as soon as possible, you'll ask yourself a question. Now what the hell should I do?"

"And?"

"You won't do anything. You'll just keep going on as before. For the moment this is all just a coincidence. These are two separate and entirely distinct matters. One is not connected with the other in any way, shape or form."

"They aren't, huh?"

"We hope," Hobart said. "We sincerely and fervently hope. Otherwise…"

I took a good slug of my beer. Hobart was in really rough shape. All the fire had gone right out of him. He had the look of a man who is fighting on the losing side and who knows it.

The envelope was hot against my chest. "Give me a hint," I said.

"It's an old, old story," Hobart said.

"Give me another hint."

Hobart didn't smile. He just stood up tiredly. "I'm sorry, kid," he said. "I've got to go. There are a lot of things still to be done…."

He left without touching his beer. I drank it because I figured the bastard owed me a couple three over the years.

It was just starting to get dark by the time I got back to the campsite with my caravan. I hooked her up, put on the coffee, had a quick shower, changed my clothes, and took my time sorting through the long plays for the turntable. All delaying tactics on my part.

The manila envelope was sitting on my desk. A small envelope that couldn't contain any more than two pages. Just two lousy pages and yet whatever was written on them had suddenly made an old man out of Hobart. I took my time finishing my first cup of coffee. Another delay.

Finally I opened it. There was one page plus a photostat of an old newspaper or magazine clipping. I put the photostat aside and moved the page under the lamp on my desk. The heading said, "A Rifleman in the Kitchen." There were a number of recipes listed below. The first was for "Roast Pheasants with Dirty Rice Annie." Very interesting. "Rub the cavities of three 2-pound pheasants with a mixture of 1 teaspoon salt and ½ teaspoon each of paprika and ground juniper berries," it instructed. "In a bowl combine 1 pound sausage meat or scrapple with 1 cup chopped mushrooms...."

I flicked the lamp switch. The white light turned off and a smaller blue one flooded the page. In this intense light a jumble of letters and figures was faintly visible between the print of the recipes. The first combination in the jumble was D2H14.

Time magazine's first issue in the previous month had *Sharon's Journey* topping the best seller list in fiction. As a result, I had purchased that novel, and now I reached for it. Chapter four, page two of that chapter, the eighth paragraph down on that page, the fourteenth word in that paragraph. The word was finger.

Before I went any further I took another look at the photostat. I still couldn't tell whether it was from a newspaper or a magazine clipping. It was quite old—*an old, old story,* Hobart had said—and the yellowing of age was apparent in the photostat.

It was a four-column photograph, a shot that had been taken with a telescopic, wide-angle lens, the cutlines under the photograph, and that's all. No text. Not that it would have helped much. The cutlines were in Russian. I should know Russian. But I don't.

Someone had marked a small arrow pointing to the head of one of the dozen or so men in the photograph. I flicked the lamp switch again, pulled open my desk drawer, and took out a magnifying glass. I held it over the face of the man with the arrow pointing at him. He looked vaguely familiar. I should know this Russian, I told myself. I should, but I don't, damn it. I went back to the recipe for "Roast Pheasants with Dirty Rice Annie."

It took me about a half-hour to decipher the message. The burden of it was that there had been three sets of prints on the martini glass that had contained the home run. Mine, the bartender's and a thumbprint—so crisp and clear that there could be absolutely no doubt—of Georgi N. Jegalova.

I knew Georgi. Or at least I knew of him. In July 1959, President Eisenhower invited Nikita Khrushchev, sometimes known as the Butcher of Budapest, to visit America. The House Committee on Un-American Activities scheduled hearings in protest. The hearings were on the "Crimes of Khrushchev." Following the hearings the committee released seven volumes charging that:

Khrushchev personally conceived and executed the mass starvation and liquidation of six to eight million Ukrainians in the early 1930's.

Khrushchev was the chief executioner for the bloody Moscow purge trials in 1936. He supervised the killing of thousands.

Khrushchev, during a second two-year reign of terror in the Ukraine in 1937–38, slaughtered another 400,000 people.

Khrushchev's postwar Ukrainian purge liquidated or exiled hundreds of thousands to slave labor camps.

Khrushchev's good right arm and most trusted killer over this bloody period was Georgi N. Jegalova.

That much I knew. But what I couldn't figure was what Georgi's thumbprint was doing on my martini glass. My hand was shaking slightly as I reached for the photostat of the four-column photograph with the small arrow pointing to the vaguely familiar Russian.

The arrow meant that this was Georgi. I took out the magnifying glass again. I was a long time with it. The face was familiar all right. Vaguely familiar.

Finally it was all very clear. I had known him for a couple of weeks. Just the two weeks and I had regretted all the years that had gone before. Well, hello there, and how's by you, H. H. Goding?

I could remember every detail of how it had happened. The bartender had handed me my martini. H. H. Goding had regarded the size of it with open admiration. He had reached for it, his hand touching mine, and I had pulled away, thinking he had missed. But he had somehow got a thumb against the glass. It was just one of those things. The white knight had got sloppy. He had sent in a glass with too many prints.

Now what? Just a coincidence? Two entirely separate and distinct matters? Oh, sure, Hobart. Sure ....

I got up and went over to the stove and turned up the main burner. I destroyed the recipes first and then the photostat. The photostat went up very quickly. Roasted pheasants. Georgi N. Jegalova. Dirty Rice Annie. H. H. Goding.

"Fantastic," I said. Then I did something really stupid. I had four very large and very potent martinis.

She came to me in the night. You could hear her coming from a long way off. Her car radio was playing much too loudly and every once in a while she would let out a war whoop.

I rolled over and turned on the light and looked at my watch. It was a little before midnight. I'd been asleep for less than two hours. That hadn't done me a damn bit of good. I was still slightly drunk. Not falling down drunk. Just lippy drunk.

I sat up, considered getting dressed, and settled instead for a robe over my pajamas. It cuts quite a figure in a low-key way. There is a little doodad embroidered over the heart. A sparrow.

The car screeched to a halt outside the caravan. The motor was switched off. The radio was turned up, a mistake, obviously, and then off. A door opened and slammed.

"Okay, come on out, J. Edgar," she called. "You hear me? You come to hell out of there. You come out or I'm coming in...."

I put on the coffee.

"J. Edgar," she shouted. "Do you hear me?" There was a long pause, a few lines of song, some mild swear words, a particularly spine-chilling war whoop, the cry of pain a person makes on stubbing a toe.

I set two cups out on the table.

"Come on, open up, you dirty fink," she screamed. She was pounding on the caravan door now. Really hammering at it.

"It's unlocked," I said. That was useless. I waited for the pounding to stop. "It's *unlocked*."

I didn't like that J. Edgar. I didn't like it at all. I wasn't FBI, maybe, but she was close enough, and that was all that mattered. The jig-a-jig-jig was up. Finished. Over.

The door pushed open slowly.

"Hi," she hicupped. "I'm sorry. You're not a fink. You're just a fink about one thing. Otherwise you are a non-finky sort...."

"That's all right," I said.

"Really," she said. "You're not and I'm sorry and I apologize pro-pro-pro..."

"Profusely."

"That also," she said. "It was a terrible thing for me to say. Actually, I'm very broken up, you know? I came just as soon as I heard. Terrible news, wasn't it? A tragedy ...."

"Enter," I told her. "Come in. I was thinking of serving coffee."

"*Coffee,*" she said. She made a face. "You know, that's just like you, J. Edgar. Maybe you are a fink after all. Only you would think of serving coffee at a time like this."

"What do you want?"

"A drink." She considered releasing her hold on the doorjamb.

"You don't need a drink," I said.

She looked down her nose at me. "I didn't say I needed a drink. I said I *wanted* a drink."

I shrugged. What the hell? She was already long gone. One more wasn't going to make any difference.

"What's the matter with you anyway, J. Edgar?" she demanded. "*Coffee.* Coffee at a time like this ...." She let go of the doorjamb and made her way unsurely to the lone easy chair. She reached it, twisted around, and sprawled backwards, her back-side just catching the edge. "Woooomph!" she yelled.

"What kind of a drink?"

She regarded me severely. "What *is* the matter with you? You know darn well I never drink anything but bourbon."

I mixed a bourbon for her and a martini for myself. I gave it to her and stood staring down at her.

"Thanks, J. Edgar," she said. "I came just as soon as I heard. Terrible news, wasn't it? A tragedy ...."

"I'm glad you came," I told her.

She took a sip of her drink. It dribbled down her chin and she leaned forward swiftly. The reflex action of a woman who didn't want it to drip onto her expensive dress. "Damn."

I found myself staring at her half-exposed breasts. She caught me at it.

"Uh, uh," she said, waggling a finger. "Naughty, naughty. I'm ashamed of you, J. Edgar. Don't you remember our vow?"

"I remember," I said. Those God damn files Morley sent me. She wasn't saying J. Edgar. She was saying Jay Edgar.

"Terrible news," she said. "Terrible, terrible news. I just couldn't accept it at first."

"Terrible," I agreed. The dashing young captain's name had been Lamberth. Jay E. Lamberth, the file had said, and the E., obviously, stood for Edgar.

"I never thought they'd nail you," she said. "I was so sure that you of all people would make it. I still can't believe they killed you, my darling, my love. My one and only Jay Edgar."

I stood staring down at her. I wasn't Charlie Sparrow. I was a dashing young captain in the infantry. Captain Jay E. Lamberth, aged twenty-four, a nice guy, bright, ambitious and promising. A very nice guy, indeed, I was, because I had made a vow, and the vow was not to do it with the exquisite, very, very sexy, very quick princess.

"A tragedy," Lisa said.

"Yes," I told her. That was some vow we had made. Not to do it until I came marching home. Only I hadn't made it home. They had nailed me of all people. I had got zapped in Viet Nam. I was dead.

I stood staring down at her and she sat staring up at me. She was Lisa Marshall. I was Jay Edgar. She was drunk as a hoot owl. I was dead. She was exquisite, very, very sexy, and quick. I'd had one too many martinis. She was a princess. I was the white knight. She was a dirty whore. I was Charlie Sparrow.

"You're a ghost," Lisa said.

"And you're the king's daughter."

There was no stopping it then. I pulled her up to me, held her, caressed her, kissed her. Kissed her father's marvelously deep liquid green eyes. The finely chiseled nose with just enough pug. The wide, full, slightly pouting mouth glistening with hot wet invitation. I kissed her eyes, and her nose, and her mouth, and I kissed the hair the color of ripe bananas.

"Take me, please," she whispered.

Why the hell not? She wasn't a princess. She was a dirty whore.

I picked her up and carried her to the bunk. Her clothes felt good in my hands. So very good and so very expensive. Clothes that smelled of smart shops and rare perfume and twelve-year-old bourbon whisky. So very good. And so very, very expensive.

Her body was nice. There was a lithe boyishness about her, but she was all woman where she was supposed to be, in the softness of her throat, in the fullness of her breasts, in the away-we-go roll of her hips. It was all very nice and if I was God I wouldn't change a damn thing.

She pulled my head up. Her mouth trembled against mine. The words came in a harsh cry. "Do *it!*"

Why not?

There was no stopping it, no turning back, no altering of course. We were both so quick. We were sheet lightning and we were falling stars. We were Lisa and Jay Edgar and we had waited too long to break our vow.

Her tears were hot against my face. There could have been a lot of reasons for those tears. Many, many reasons why she should be crying now. But we both knew there was only one reason and that she would cry this way only the one time. Only the once.

Lisa was a virgin.

CHAPTER SIX

It was four o'clock in the morning by the time I got her back to the Casa Alegre. She was a very worn-out princess, because we hadn't slept that much, maybe two hours at the most, locked in each other's arms, drunk, spent and content. We could have stayed that way for days if it wasn't for the demons that came to plague me after those two hours of blissful sleep.

The demons had poked me awake. They had poked me with their pitchforks and they had reminded me that while my bunk may have been in Heaven, it was perched right on the edge, ready to topple off at any moment, and that below burned the fires of Hell. Maggie Hilton was Doris Dubois. H. H. Goding was Georgi N. Jegalova. Lisa, my Lisa, really was a princess, not a dirty whore. Nobody, it seemed, was who they were supposed to be, nothing made sense any more, and the honeymoon was over.

I kissed her good night on the portal.

" 'Bye, date," she said.

That wasn't as cold as it sounded. We had said what we had to say as I drove her into town in her Buick. I had said I was sorry, and she had said she was glad, and I had said I was glad, too, but now what the hell do we do, and she had grinned and said we do the same thing again tomorrow night, silly. So the 'bye, date, wasn't cold at all, but just an inside joke. Or something.

I saw her in, heard the lock click, tossed the car keys under the front seat of the Buick, and went for a walk through the narrow streets of Alamos. Dogs barked at me. Burros regarded me as an absolute idiot. A pig came along with me for the last two blocks.

My destination was a casita, or small house, on the south side of the town, which had only been recently invaded by Americans. It was at the end of its street and balanced precariously on the edge of a stone wall guarding against arroyo flooding. It didn't appear too permanent but it was rumored to be one of the oldest buildings in Alamos.

I knocked on the door. A light clicked on somewhere out back. There was a short wait and then the door creaked open a few inches.

"May we come in?" I asked.

"Jesus," Tyler said. He let me in. He told the pig to scram.

I followed him back to the kitchen and he put on a pot of coffee. I had never been in his casa before. It was very small, built in miniature almost, and he moved about the kitchen clumsily, a giant in a dollhouse.

"Why did you take this?"

"Only thing available," he grumbled.

We sat down and waited for the coffee to perk. The table was only a yard square. The chairs belonged in Grade One.

"Who owns it? Midgets?"

"The Seven Dwarfs."

I offered him one of my Viceroys. He took it and we both lit up. "Well?" he asked.

"I'm scared," I said.

"Of whom? Georgi Porgi?"

"That was bad enough," I said. "But the bottom really fell out tonight. Lisa came out to the caravan."

His eyes narrowed. "And?"

"And she was drunk."

He sat waiting for me to finish.

"She was very drunk," I said. "She kept calling me Jay Edgar. That was the captain's name. Jay Edgar Lamberth."

He was really angry now. His jaw was set and a nerve was twitching near the corner of his mouth.

"You didn't have a chance," I said. "Morley left an important fact out of her file. Lamberth looked a lot like me. A striking resemblance."

I could see he hadn't known that. His eyes widened and the harsh line of his mouth parted. "He looked like you?"

"Yes," I said. "That's why Marshall took such an interest in me. I was a ghost from the past and a possible solution to his problem with Lisa. It seems he wants her settled down before he embarks on his campaign for the presidency. So he dragged her down here with the idea that after the shock wore off she would start up where she left off two years ago."

Tyler shook his head. "That's too far out."

"I thought so, too," I said. "But Morley thought it would work, and so, obviously, did Marshall. It was far out but it was worth a try and so he brought her down here .…"

Tyler was still shaking his head.

"You were just a backstop," I said. "The understudy. You weren't supposed to come on unless the star couldn't make it. So don't feel too badly—as it turned out, you just didn't have a chance, lover boy."

Tyler laughed softly. "That God damn Morley."

"Oh, he's cute, all right," I said. "He told us just enough and that's all. If the girl comes down, compete for her, and may the best man win."

Tyler wasn't angry any more. He had his pride back now. The dice had been loaded against him. Under normal circumstances, he was telling himself, he would have been the best man, not Charlie Sparrow. The part I didn't like was that he probably was right.

"So what happened?" Tyler demanded. He had that leering grin pasted on his face. The man is a sex maniac.

The coffee was ready. I indicated my empty cup. He got up impatiently and poured it.

"You know all that razzle-dazzle in Lisa's updated file?" I said. "When the captain got killed, she really went around the bend, put out for every guy in the Army, from buck private up?"

"Sure," Tyler laughed. "The enlistment rate doubled. Two more like her and they could have done away with the draft."

"No," I said. "The file is a phony. That's all a bunch of crap."

Tyler snorted. "Lisa told you, huh?"

"That's right," I said. "And I believe her, not Morley, Tyler. Lisa came to me tonight as a virgin."

Tyler looked as if he had been hit in the face with a railroad tie. "You're sure?" he asked finally.

I nodded.

"A guy can be fooled...."

"Not this guy," I said. "There are three kinds of virgins: Are you kidding? Well, maybe, baby, just maybe. And *virgins.*"

"Okay, okay," Tyler said. He was angry again. Not much, but angry, and you couldn't blame him for that, I thought. "You was there, Charlie."

"That's why I'm scared," I told him. "Maggie Hilton is Doris Dubois. H. H. Goding is Georgi N. Jegalova. Lisa is, or was, a virgin, and now I'm seriously beginning to wonder, is Marshall really Marshall?"

"What are you smoking?" Tyler asked.

"Viceroys," I said. I offered him another. He didn't think that was funny.

"I'm fairly amenable," I said. "I can accept most things up to a point. There's usually a pretty good reason why things are done the way they are done. But I come to the end of my ball of string when they promise me a whore and give me a virgin."

Tyler thought about that for a while. I could practically see the gears turning. He thought about it but he didn't have any answer.

"Let us consider various possibilities," I said. "Morley is a Russian spy. So is Hobart. So, perhaps, are you."

Tyler shook his head. "I don't buy that."

"All right," I said. "Then the boys who checked out Lisa got their facts wrong. People fed them a lot of crap and they accepted it. Ruined a poor girl's reputation."

He shook his head again. "Never happen."

"It's a fake file? Not from Morley?"

"Hardly."

"That leaves one of two things," I said. "The first is very hard to figure. Morley did more than omit some pertinent facts in Lisa's file. He purposely put in a bunch of lies to make us think Lisa was one of the world's easiest flops. Do you buy that?"

"No," Tyler said. "Why should he do that? It doesn't make any sense. Let's face it, I'm going to work twice as hard, and I mean *twice* as hard, to tumble with a girl who has never been in the gym before."

"Me, too," I admitted.

He sucked at his teeth. He was trying to think of the last possibility. He's a pretty good guy, a great lover and all that, but he does not get S for Smart.

"Okay," I said. "Do you buy this: Lisa is *not* Lisa?"

He took one of my cigarettes. "Viceroys, huh?"

I waited for more than that.

"There's an explanation," he said.

Sure, I thought. There's an explanation for everything. Only we didn't have it. I finished my coffee and made up my mind.

"Where are you going?"

"We are," I said. "Into Navojoa. I'm going to call Morley."

He looked doubtful. "Can't you go alone?"

"I need your car."

"So take it."

"Thanks," I said. "But if I take it, I may not bring it back, Tyler."

"You have other plans?"

"Maybe."

The doubting look was still there. "I don't think the two of us should go running off. What about Georgi?"

"Every hotel in town is booked solid," I said tiredly. "Did it ever occur to you why so many tourists showed up so suddenly last night?"

"How did you know about the hotels?"

"I didn't," I said. "I just guessed. When I read the recipes, I just guessed we'd be getting a lot of tourists, and I just guessed their way would be paid by Uncle Sam."

"That's probably it," Tyler agreed.

I grinned at him. "You buy that one, huh?"

He went to change and I went outside to wait. The sky was much blacker than it had been when I had walked over from the Casa Alegre. Dark clouds were gathering and they were threatening rain.

I looked at my watch. It was 4:22. We'd be in Navojoa well before five o'clock. While I was looking, a raindrop splattered against the face of my watch, bigger than hell, and I decided I'd better get under cover. I crossed the street to Tyler's Chevy.

The damn door was stuck as usual. I was standing there, pulling at it, when something was pushed against my right kidney, flat and hard. It felt very much like a rod.

"Okay," Ace King whispered. "Now, just come along quietly. Come on, move it, and act natural."

We started down the street. It was a short block with only three houses to the corner. Once around that, we'd be out of sight, lost in a maze of ruins, and Tyler wouldn't know where to look first. The rod jabbed harder.

I tried to think it out. Once they took me, it would be easy, real easy, to take Tyler. He would just walk right out into their hands. Then there would be no one left to tell Morley about my unique experience with Lisa.

Ace had to go. I bent my right wrist. A small cylinder dropped down from its holder into the palm of my hand. I had to turn it around, because the nozzle was pointing the wrong way, but that just took a second, and now it was aimed straight at him. My thumb was rubbing against the firing pin.

"This is easier than I thought," Ace laughed.

I stopped and turned around to face him. He had a rod, all right, a fishing rod, and like he had said, the next time it rained he was coming to get me.

"Not this morning," I told him.

"I didn't think so," he grinned. "You and Tyler, you've been out on the town, huh?"

"That's right."

"Just going to bed?"

"Yes."

He rubbed his nose. "Well, maybe next time, Charlie. I better get going. Dutch'll be waiting for me."

"Lots of luck," I said. I stood and watched him lope off down the street to Dutch's. He'd already had more luck that morning than any man deserved. If he hadn't laughed then, just at that precise moment, I'd have pressed that damn pin, and no more Ace King.

I walked back and got into the Chevy. Tyler came out of the house a couple of minutes later and pushed behind the wheel. I must have been still pretty white around the gills, because Tyler, who doesn't usually notice these things, remarked upon it.

We made it to Navojoa, a thirty-two-mile drive over a good paved road, most of it fairly straight, in just over half an hour. The rain stopped as soon as we twisted down out of the hills and then it was all clear driving on the flatlands. Tyler couldn't really open up, though, because the fences aren't all that good along the road, and you never know when you're going to meet up with some livestock.

That time of morning, not yet five, the one telephone circuit going up to the border at Nogales was open and waiting, and it was less than ten minutes after placing the call that I was talking to Morley. He was at home. It was going on seven in Washington.

"What do you think you're doing?" Morley asked.

"Telephoning," I said. "From Navojoa."

There was a noise on the line. A crunchy static.

"So the operator said. You're off base."

I explained what he already knew. The only places with phones in Alamos were the hotels. The hotels had switchboards and the operators might be nosey.

"All right," he said.

I was still hearing that crunchy static.

"Listen," I said. "Are you eating toast?"

"Cinnamon," he told me. "For breakfast. It is breakfast time."

I waited until he had finished.

"You know this girl I like?" I said then. "Well, I took her for a ride last night, and she went all the way."

"That's nice," he said.

"I thought so, too," I admitted. "Only I thought you might like to know something. She had never been that route before."

There was a long silence. Morley's voice was much clearer now. "Can the double-talk."

"I laid her," I said.

"I got that part."

"You also got the other part," I said. "She had never been laid before. Not by anybody."

There was another silence. Longer this time. "You're sure?"

"Yes," I said. Everybody was asking me if I was sure. "No mistake about it. Very, very sure. Positive."

"That can't be," Morley said.

"That's too bad," I told him. "But it's true. You want me to mail you the sheets?"

Morley took another bite of toast. "Tyler with you?"

"Yes."

"Put him on."

I motioned to Tyler to come to the booth. He was inside only for a moment. Then we changed places again.

I put my hand over the speaker. "What did he say?"

"He asked if you were drunk."

"What did you tell him?"

Tyler grinned. I shut the door in his face.

"Tyler says you are sober," Morley said.

"He had to say that," I said. "I have a gun on him."

Morley chewed toast for a while. That wasn't a very good sign. Usually he thinks pretty fast.

"I don't know what to think," Morley said.

That sort of snapped it for me. Morley is a genius. He has the papers to prove it.

"There can be no doubt about that file, huh?" I asked.

"None whatsoever."

"You know what that means?"

"I know what that means."

I took a deep breath. "This girl isn't that girl."

There was no reply.

"Only her father says she *is*."

"I gathered that much," he said absently.

I waited for something else. He remained silent.

"Well?" I asked.

"This is going to take some time," he said. There was a pause. That meant he was looking at his watch.

"You want me to call you back?"

"Yes."

"When?"

"A couple of hours. No, make it three hours."

"You want to hear a real crazy idea?" I asked.

"Try me."

"If we've got the wrong girl, could we have the wrong father, too?"

"How could that be?"

"I don't know," I said. "How good is the file on him? How good is it and how far does it go back?"

"It's a good file," Morley said. "It goes all the way back to when he was in the Army. Long before the girl was born. Besides, you can't change fingerprints, or hadn't you heard?"

Fingerprints. What in the hell was the matter with me?

"I'll get the girl's today," I said.

"Don't bother."

"Don't *bother*?"

"Nothing to check them against," Morley said agreeably.

"You mean she's never been printed?"

"Never."

"How about feet? You know, on some birth certificates…"

"Never," Morley said. "Any other ideas?"

"You're sure about that file?"

"It's a good file."

"I'm not convinced," I said.

"Three hours," Morley said. He hung up.

I slowly replaced the phone on the hook. How did Morley know it was such a damn good file? If he was feeding me such great files, why hadn't somebody noted—just a one-line explanation—why Doris Dubois, alias Maggie Hilton, had quit her job, voluntarily, on a Wednesday? There could be all kinds of explanations for her doing that. A million of them. But if it was a good file, a really good file, prepared by a top pro, there would be that explanation.

Oh, you're so God damn smart, Morley, but you've blown a few in your time, and you just might blow this one. You're not the only genius in the world.

Tyler pulled open the door of the booth. "Well?"

"Morley wants me to take a little trip," I said.

"You sure?"

I put a hand over my face to indicate my despair. "No. I'm lying, Tyler."

He inclined his head. "What about back there?"

"Morley says you're to hold the fort. I'll be back tomorrow."

"Where are you going?"

"To check on an Easter card."

That didn't ring a bell with him. Sure, Morley. All our files are great. The files are great because we hire only real sharpies.

"I don't get it," Tyler said.

I was tired, I was scared stiff, I was crossing Morley for the first time in my life, and Tyler didn't get it. Screw you, Tyler.

CHAPTER SEVEN

I took off from Navojoa shortly after six o'clock in a chartered Beechcraft Musketeer Sport III. No flight plan. The pilot was too sleepy to know where he was going and too tired to care. I had a road map in my lap and gave him the directions from that. All he said the whole flight, once for each proposed alteration in course, was *"Si."*

He didn't know English and I'm not exactly fluent in Spanish. I know enough to limp along and that's all. I think that I shall never si. Yes will have to do for me. We flew east back towards Alamos, veering slightly south, skirting the rain clouds packed against the hills there, and then kept pushing east until we picked up the railway coming up from San Blas. From there we turned north and followed the tracks along Copper Canyon and across the Continental Divide to Ciudad Guerrero. Then east again and followed Highway 16 to Ojinaga on the Rio Grande.

I left the plane there. *"Quede usted aqui,"* I told the pilot. *"Regresare mañana."*

"Si," he said. He heaved his bulk back and closed his eyes.

That was a good sign. I apparently had gotten it right. He apparently understood.

I took a taxi across the border into Presidio and put in a call to Morley. It had been about a 400-mile flight. The Sport III has a maximum speed of 140. We had averaged roughly 120. I was more than slightly late making the call.

"So you decided to play games?" Morley said.

"Yes," I said. "What have you decided?"

There was a long pause. "We haven't."

I waited through another one.

"You're absolutely sure about the virginity bit?" Morley asked.

"Yes."

"Any girl who has had an abortion can't be a virgin."

"I know that."

"We've had the doctor on the grill this morning," Morley said. "There's no doubt there. She had an abortion."

"I had the girl in my bunk last night," I said. "There's no doubt there, either. You're sure you don't want to do my laundry?"

He ignored that. "Yet it's the same girl?" he asked.

"She says she is. Her father says she is. Everybody around the house accepts her. The special assistant, the accountant, the secretary...."

"And her photographs?"

"She looks like she looks in her photographs. A little more beautiful, if that's possible, but she's the girl in the pictures, all right."

"Maybe it's plastic surgery?"

That was really reaching. "Come on," I said. "She wasn't wearing any sort of mask. Everything she had on, I took off, *sir*."

Morley made a blowing noise. It sounded as if he was back on cigarettes. "There's something wrong," he said.

"That's what I've been telling you."

"There's something wrong with the file."

"*Exactly* what I've been telling you."

"We'll have to go over the whole thing."

"Thanks."

He made that same kind of noise. I was sure of it now. Back on the weed.

"So you are going to Easter?" Morley said.

"Yes."

"How long will you be?"

"Just the day."

He sighed. "All right then."

"You mean it's okay with you?"

"No," he said. "I mean I don't really blame you."

"That helps a little."

"Then I withdraw the statement."

"Twins," I said. "How much do you bet it's twins?"

"Of course," Morley said. "When this is over, we'll get you a good psychiatrist, my son. In the meantime, call me, will you?" He hung up.

I had steak and eggs for breakfast, rented an aging Ford, and took off over the mountains on U.S. 67, first stop sixty miles north at the county seat, Marfa. I stopped at the courthouse there and checked some old records and picked up a Xerox copy of a birth certificate. Then twenty miles northwest on U.S. 90 to Easter. The Ford got me there going on two o'clock.

I had expected a bit more. It was a lower-case *s* small town, a couple of blocks of false fronts on either side of the highway, the main industry gas stations, the main attraction the water tower. Population several hundred at most.

The sheriff's office was a block back off the highway on what was once the main drag. On a corner in a one-story adobe-style whitewashed-brick building that looked old and decrepit enough to be of some slight historical significance. Next-door was a frame building with a big window in front. The glass was cracked and there was just a trace left of fancy black-on-gold letters that spelled out DRYG ODS. There weren't any dryg ods behind the window. The store was vacant. Next-door to that was a laundry. It was closed. Busy town.

"Trouble?" the deputy asked. He was the long, lean type, weathered, knowing. There was a white patch over the left pocket of his blue denim jacket. "Lattimore," was stenciled on it. He was leaning back in a rickety chair with his cowboy boots propped up on an old iron pot-bellied stove. The chair was balanced precariously and the door to the stove was open for the warmth of a few coals that glowed dully.

"Not me," I said. I handed him my wallet opened to the card stating I was a senior editor of *Time* magazine.

He read that and the rest of the cards, enjoyed the photographs of the girls, took a peek at the extent of my worldly wealth, and then handed the wallet back. "An editor, huh?"

"A writer, really," I said. I sat down in the other chair and pulled open the stove door a bit wider. "You ever hear of a Davis Marshall?"

"I'm just a deputy," he said.

"No," I said. "That's this man's name. Mr. Marshall. Mr. Davis Marshall."

"Marshall?"

"Yes."

He regarded the ceiling thoughtfully. "From around these parts?"

"Yes."

"Can't say I have."

"He was born here," I said.

"Oh? When might that have been?"

"In nineteen-twenty."

"Before my time."

I gave him the Xerox copy I had picked up in Marfa. The certificate said that Davis Berwick Marshall was a male, that he had gone through a nine-month period of pregnancy, and that he had been born April 12, 1920, in Easter, Texas. The father's full name was William Hilliard Marshall, his color or race was white, he was aged twenty-two at the time of birth, his usual occupation was rancher, and he was born in Rumford, Maine. The mother's maiden name was Sarah Irene Vaughn, she was white, she was sixteen at the time, and she was born in Louisville, Georgia. The attending physician's name was Dr. Royal F. Empey.

Lattimore read it carefully and handed it back without comment.

"You know any of these people?" I asked.

The ceiling got another going over. "Why you asking?"

"Mr. Davis Marshall is quite an important person now," I said. "He's a very rich and highly respected businessman and there is talk of him running for the presidency of the United States."

"Oh?" Lattimore thought for a moment. "Not very bright, huh?"

"If he runs, we'll want to do a story on him," I said. "That's why I'm here. To get some stuff on his early childhood. What he was like as a boy, how he did in school, comments from people who knew him then. Human interest stuff…"

"Agnes," Lattimore said.

"Who?"

"Old Doc Empey's niece." Lattimore leaned forward and spat into the fire. It was my first knowledge that he had a wad in his mouth. He carried it well.

"She still lives here?"

"Yep."

"Where?"

"Up the street a piece."

"How do I get there?"

"Walk. Or you can take your car."

I offered him one of my Viceroys. He declined. "Bad for you," he said.

I ignored the warning and lit up. "You mind describing the house?"

"I was thinking of showing you," he said.

Agnes Empey lived in a weather-beaten two-story frame home with a gingerbread decorated front porch at the north end of town on the same street as the sheriff's office. It was old and fragile and it looked as if it might blow away in the next good windstorm. Agnes had the same look, a small, shriveled, button-nosed old lady wearing a dirty gray shawl and granny glasses. When Lattimore knocked, she called, "It's open," and when we entered the parlor, a dark and somehow unpleasant room from another era, she made no move to leave her rocking chair.

"This is Mr. Sparrow, Agnes," Lattimore told her. "He's from *Time* magazine. Going to write something up on one of our former citizens."

"Funny name," Agnes said. She regarded me curiously from behind the granny glasses.

Lattimore sat down and put his hat on the floor beside him. I took a cane chair from against the wall and pulled it in close.

"You remember some people lived around here called the Marshalls?" Lattimore asked.

Agnes didn't take her little bird eyes off me. "Name's familiar."

"Well," Lattimore said. He appeared to be looking for a place to spit. "It seems these Marshall people had a son, boy named Davis, back in 1920. The Doc delivered him."

"Not unusual."

"Didn't say it was, Agnes," Lattimore said soothingly. "Just asked you if you remembered these people the Marshalls. The father's name was William, William Hilliard, and the mother's name, her maiden name, was Vaughn. Sarah Irene Vaughn."

Lattimore had a good memory. He had read the birth certificate only the once.

"Marshall," Agnes said, still watching me carefully. "They be ranchers?"

"They're the ones," Lattimore said. He glanced about despairingly. "You got a place I can spit?"

"Outside," Agnes said. "Over the porch. Mind the peonies."

I stared back into the bird eyes. They seemed alert enough. But there weren't any peonies in front of the porch.

Lattimore put on his hat and went out.

"You recall the Marshalls?" I asked.

"That was a long time ago," Agnes said. "I think it was the Marshalls. Something like that anyway. They had a ranch back out of town toward the mountains. Standoffish folk, and they didn't come in much, and then only for supplies."

"Or to have a baby?"

Agnes grinned around isolated and yellowing teeth. "They had babies, they had them at the ranch, young man."

"The Doc would go out?"

"That's right."

"But he would list the birthplace as Easter?"

"Had to list something."

"Do you specifically recall William Marshall?"

"If they're the same people, that'd be Bill, the son, and he ran the ranch. He's the one who came to town. I don't recall the father's name. He was a cripple from some kind of accident."

"And the mother?"

"Dead."

"All right," I said. "You remember the son, Bill Marshall, and he had a wife, Sarah. Do you recall Sarah?"

"No."

"What about her parents? People called the Vaughns? Were they from around these parts?"

She shook her head. "No, if they were, I'd remember them for sure. I have cousins named Vaughn in Alabama. I would have looked up any people named Vaughn who came to Easter."

"So William Marshall would have married Sarah Vaughn in some place other than Easter?"

The yellow teeth showed again. "If they was rightly married."

"Yes," I said. The same thought had occurred to me. There was no record in Marfa of a marriage between a William Marshall and a Sarah Vaughn. And Sarah, at age sixteen, had been pretty young, even for those days, to be married and having a baby.

Lattimore came clomping back into the parlor. He resumed his chair and put his hat back on the floor.

"You spared the peonies?"

"Never touched a one, Agnes."

"Let's talk about their son," I said. "Bill and Sarah had a boy named Davis. He was born April 12, 1920, and Doc delivered him, right?"

"If you've seen a certificate that says so."

"You don't specifically recall this birth?"

"No."

"But surely you must recall the boy? Young Davis, he'd have to come in to town to go to school, wouldn't he?"

"What school?"

"There wasn't any school in Easter?"

She shook her head. "The closest school then would be in Valentine. That's fifteen miles north. The Marshalls was a good five miles west of Easter. If the boy got any schooling, he'd get it out of books on the ranch, I'd say."

That hardly made sense. Marshall's file said he had a high school education when he entered the U. S. Army, on December 16, 1941, in El Paso. He also had to have a good basic education to pile up almost two years of university equivalency, which the file claimed he managed during the four years he served.

"How about people on the neighboring ranches?" I asked. "The Marshalls must have had neighbors and they would have seen the boy. Are any of those people still around?"

The shriveled head shook once more. "No. Everybody pulled out of those hills years ago. The Wilsons, who stayed the longest, left sometime during the war. The boys in the service and no one left to work the place."

"Where are the Wilsons now?"

"In heaven, I trust. Both boys were killed in the war. Their father, he was an old man, and the mama, she was dying of the cancer when they left, and that be almost thirty years ago."

"Any hired hands who used to work those ranches?"

"To be paid with what?"

Lattimore picked up his hat.

"Wait a minute," I said. "Surely there must be some old-timers still around who would have known the Marshalls? They can't all be dead or gone."

The bird eyes were twinkling now behind the granny glasses. "Tell him, deputy."

"Easter has a sad past," Lattimore said. "There was an influenza epidemic here in the winter of thirty-six. It took one out of every three in town. Especially the old people."

"The Doc died then?"

"Yep. Him and a lot of others. Agnes, here, she was one of the few survivors among the old folks, and what with that and the depression and the land no good in the first place—well, those that was left just moved on, that's all."

"Scattered," Agnes said. She spit out the word.

That explained the two death certificates back in Marfa, for William and Sarah Marshall, both dated in November 1936, and both listing the cause of death as 'flu.

"The town didn't get back on its feet until after the war," Lattimore said. He grinned sheepishly. "By your standards, I guess it ain't taken many steps, huh?"

"Hold on," I said. "Let me get this straight. You mean Agnes is the only person who lived here during the thirties who is still around?"

"There's Billie."

"*Billie*," Agnes said. "Mind is gone. Rotting in the old folks home in Valentine."

"How about Hershey?" Lattimore suggested.

"He came during the war."

Lattimore shrugged. "Sorry. That's it for sure. Everybody else came either during the war or after. I know that for a fact. Came then myself."

"Thank you," I told Agnes. "Sorry to have troubled you. I'll be getting along now."

"I enjoy visitors," Agnes said. She leaned back contentedly and the bird eyes shut abruptly behind the granny glasses.

I stopped at the door. There was a table there with a Bible. I opened the cover to the first page. There was a dedication and a signature scrawled across it. "To Agnes," it said. "My good right hand in God's work." It was signed "Royal F. Empey."

I checked that signature against the one on the birth certificate. They were the same. No doubt about it.

"Watch the peonies," Agnes said.

"I will," I promised. I followed Lattimore out onto the porch and down into the dusty street that had once been the main drag of Easter.

Lattimore let me use the telephone in his office. I talked to the principals of both the elementary and the high school in Valentine. They had the records going all the way back, they were extremely co-operative, and neither school ever had a pupil named Davis Marshall. There were no telephone listings for a Marshall in Easter, Valentine or Marfa. Nor were there any Vaughns.

"You're a writer, huh?" Lattimore asked.

"That's right," I said.

He moved his wad. "You act more like a cop. A cop who's come to a brick wall."

"You think so?"

"Yep."

"You're wrong."

"Been wrong before," he said agreeably.

Back in the Ford I started sorting out the results of my day's work. A boy named Davis Berwick Marshall had been born April 12, 1920, in Easter, Texas, to a William Marshall and a Sarah

Vaughn. That there was no doubt about. The doctor's signature checked with the one in the Bible.

William and Sarah may or may not have been married. The likelihood was that they were not. That would explain why they were standoffish and why only William, never Sarah, never the boy, Davis, came in to Easter. Shame kept the unwed mother and the good-looking bastard son back in the hills.

But was shame enough to deny a boy proper schooling? That was stretching it too far. But maybe it wasn't just shame. Maybe it was a combination of shame and simple economics. Agnes had explained the financial situation with her remark about hired hands. *To be paid with what?*

If they couldn't afford to send the boy to school, they wouldn't want him showing up in town, people asking questions, maybe causing trouble. So they would keep him in the hills. And who says he was denied proper schooling?

They could at least buy him books. Sarah could act as his teacher. Hell, back in the late twenties, early thirties, that probably was a common solution in remote rural areas, and so what was so strange about this particular case? And perhaps Davis managed to go to school somewhere in the period between when his parents died and when he joined the Army.

William and Sarah had died in 1936. Davis would be sixteen, old enough to be on his own, capable of working and going to school at night, and there really was no reason to believe he lied when he claimed a high school education upon entering the Army. But the trouble with the file was that it didn't say *where* he went to school. It just accepted that part as fact.

Marshall's file began, really, on December 16, 1941, in El Paso. The day he joined the Army. The day he was first fingerprinted. He was easy to follow then because everything was laid out for you. It was a matter of public record. What he did in the service, the university education he obtained there and afterwards, his outstanding success in business, his steady rise to such a position of prominence that he could now go after—and quite possibly attain—the presidency of the United States.

Yes, he was really easy to follow, all right—*after* December 16, 1941. But before that? Well, all I knew, for certain, was that he had been born. I couldn't find anyone who knew him as a boy or a young man. There had to be people who knew him then, of course, especially after he left home when his parents died, when he finally went out into the big wide world. But in order to get the names of those people I was going to have to ask Marshall. Somebody was going to have to ask him. Somebody was going to have to say, "Listen, fellow, what the hell goes, huh?"

The decision as to who asked those embarrassing questions would be up to Morley.

Lattimore had said there was a brick wall. Well, that's how much you know, deputy. They haven't built a brick wall yet that you can't loosen a few bricks. All you have to do is keep scratching at the mortar. Even a fingernail will do if you have the time.

I was a couple of miles out of town, heading back to Marfa, when I noticed the pickup truck in my rear-view mirror, closing very fast. It looked like a Chevrolet half-ton. The driver the only occupant.

He was in a really big hurry, so I slowed and drew over a bit to let him pass. I wasn't paying that much attention, because my mind was on Marshall, mulling over the blacked-out years of his life, and that was a mistake on my part.

The driver of the pickup came alongside. He had a cap pulled down low, he was wearing sunglasses, he had a silk stocking pulled over his face, and he was pointing a grenade launcher straight at me.

I ducked. There was a whoosh, the grenade slammed over my head, banged against the far door, and then bounced back into my lap. That is a lovely place to have a live grenade.

I picked it up and dropped it out the window. It exploded a fraction of a second later. The rear end of the Ford picked up a hell of a lot of shrapnel. I got a couple shreds myself.

The Ford started bucking. I turned off the key, fought with the wheel a while, and finally rolled to a stop at the side of the road. By that time the pickup was long gone. A speck in the distance.

First, I made sure I was going to live. Then I got out and inspected the other damage. The left rear tire was flat and the gas tank was leaking in several places. I had just started to change the tire when the roar of a truck engine disturbed me. I took one quick look down the highway and headed for the ditch. My friend was coming back.

He went by at about eighty and the two shots I got away didn't even come close. Then the red lights told me that he was braking. I scrambled back onto the road for the cover of the Ford.

He got out on the driver's side, putting a wall of steel between him and my peashooter, and it occurred to me that he was just going to squat there, set up his God damn grenade launcher, and then go pow, pow, pow. I headed back for the ditch.

There was a whoosh and I flattened out and covered my head. The Ford took what sounded like a direct hit. Glass tinkled down around me.

I got up, took exactly five steps, and dived headfirst into a culvert. The second whoosh came at the same time. The explosion that followed was much too close for comfort.

I started elbowing my way along the culvert. Two more grenades hit the ditch in rapid succession. The son of a bitch sure wasn't taking any chances.

Okay, I told myself. If you get a clear shot, what say you kill him, huh? Anybody that mean deserves to die.

I slipped out of the culvert and peeked over the edge of the ditch. The pickup was again long gone. Barely visible down the highway.

He was lucky, I thought. Very, very lucky. There was no way of him knowing about the culvert. If he had just hung around a minute longer, I would have come out behind him, on the other side of the highway, and he would have been a sitting duck.

Lucky. So very lucky. But then I was lucky, too. I called it even and walked back to take a look at the Ford.

It was a mess. All the windows were blasted out. The body looked like somebody had spent a week banging it with a sledge-hammer. Two more tires were flat. The rubber was knocked right off one of the wheels.

I tried the ignition. For some reason, the motor still ran, but it was thinking of committing suicide any moment. I said to hell with it and sat down to wait.

A car came along about five minutes later. It stopped and an old geezer in a peaked cap and windbreaker surveyed the situation with a certain amount of dissatisfaction. "You hit something?" he asked.

"Yeah," I said. "A rabbit. He went away limping, I'll tell you."

"Texans," he grumbled. That's when I noticed his license plate. He was from Vermont.

He drove me back into Easter. We didn't talk much. I asked him what he was doing in Texas. He said he was driving around the South waiting for it to get cold in Vermont. In Vermont, he said, they had nine months of winter, followed by three months of cold weather.

He dropped me off at the side of the highway in Easter. I told him I didn't want him to go out of his way. He said he didn't have any intention of going out of his way.

I walked the two blocks to the old weather-beaten house with the gingerbread and the non-existent peonies. Agnes was still sitting in her rocking chair. Her bird eyes had a strange stare to them behind the granny glasses. I sighed. Maybe they had peonies where she was now.

Lattimore was sitting beside her with his hat on the floor. "Trouble," he said.

"What happened?" I asked.

The wad moved imperceptibly. "I was thinking of asking you."

CHAPTER EIGHT

Mother always told me to never argue with a policeman. Just go along quietly, tell the whole truth and nothing but the truth, and the worst that can happen to you, son, is you'll get the electric chair. Mother was quite a philosopher. One who met all events with calmness and composure.

"You're bleeding," Lattimore said.

"I know," I told him. "A grenade. I was about two miles up the road when this pickup pulled alongside. The driver had a silk stocking over his face and he..."

"And he threw a grenade in your car?"

"Not exactly. He had a grenade launcher and he fired it right in my face. I ducked and it slammed against the far door of the car and then bounced back into my lap."

"So you picked it up and tossed it out and just got a few shreds in your arm?"

"Yeah."

Lattimore stood up tiredly. He pulled a pair of cuffs off his belt. He swung them in the standard fashion. So much for the truth.

I put up my left wrist to accept the cuff. He banged it around and it snapped tightly. I pulled down then, yanking him toward me, and poked two rigid fingers in his eyes, hard enough to make him think he had been blinded.

He was easy to take then. A knee in the crotch and another under his jaw as he bent over. His head snapped back sharply and he went down and out.

I took his keys, freed my cuffed wrist, put the handcuffs on him, dragged him into the kitchen, and stuffed him bound and gagged in the pantry. I stole his gun and his badge and his hat and his jacket. Then I went outside and stole his car.

The sign was flapping in the breeze at the side of the highway about four miles south of Valentine. "Burden's End," it said, and below that, in smaller letters, "All Visitors Must Check at Front Desk." I turned in between two fieldstone pillars and drove down a willow-lined white gravel road.

The entrance was great, but the place itself looked like a rather shabby hotel, the kind frequented by commercial travelers who aren't making their sales quota that year. The porch was set with about a dozen rocking chairs in a neat row. They were all empty. Nap time.

I went inside and checked at the front desk. A horsey type in a nurse's cap, moth-holed pink sweater and a crinkled print housedress, decorated with daisies, looked up at me over a copy of *Real Love Adventures*.

"I'm Coombs," I said. I flashed Lattimore's badge.

She stared at me without comprehension.

"I called only twenty minutes ago," I said. "I made arrangements to visit with one of your patients. Billie."

"I know," she said.

"Well?"

She put down her magazine and stood up unsurely. "There was a man here saying he was you only five minutes ago," she said. "He took Billie into Marfa. Said he wanted her to look at some pictures. For identification or something."

"Her?"

"What do you mean?"

"Billie is a she? A woman?"

"Of course."

I decided I needed a cigarette. I lit it slowly, thinking about brick walls, and how easy it is to scratch away the mortar if you have the time. "This officer said he was me?"

"He said he was the police. I assumed it was you. You had just called and then he came around and..."

"Any identification?"

"No. I just assumed..." Her mouth started to sag. "Is anything wrong?"

"I'm not sure," I lied. "This officer? Can you describe him?"

"Well," she said. "He was tall. An older man. Wearing glasses."

"What color hair?"

"Dark. Sort of brownish. I'm not really sure."

I looked at her copy of *Real Love Adventures*. "Handsome?"

"No," she said. "I wouldn't say that. His nose was too long and he had sort of squinty eyes."

"Anything else? Mustache? Scars? Moles? Birthmarks? That sort of thing?"

"A scar."

"Where?"

She pointed. "This side of his mouth. It was small but noticeable."

"Teeth," I said. "His own or store-bought?"

She laughed. "I think he bought them."

"Anything else?"

"I don't think so."

"Okay," I said. "Now, about his truck..."

"It wasn't a truck," she said immediately. "It was a car and fairly new. I didn't pay that much attention but I think it was a Dodge. A late model dark blue Dodge."

"And he was taking Billie into Marfa?"

"That's what he said."

Like hell. No dark blue Dodge had passed me. He must be heading north and by now he was past Valentine. "May I use your phone?" I asked.

"Sure."

I phoned the sheriff's office in Valentine. I told the character who answered that I was an FBI agent working on a very important case and that I had reason to believe that a late model dark blue Dodge with a kidnap victim from Burden's End was traveling north on U.S. 90 between Valentine and Van Horn. I got an argument but I finally convinced this doubting character that he should arrange for a roadblock south of Van Horn. I'd be along in a few minutes, we'd argue about it then, and there was no harm done if I was a phony, I said. But if I wasn't a phony and he didn't have that roadblock up—well, his ass would be in a sling, wouldn't it?

"FBI?" Real Love Adventure gasped. "I thought you were from the sheriff's office?"

I showed her a card I hadn't shown Lattimore. That satisfied her I was FBI. She ought to have been satisfied. It was the real thing. Well, it was, and then again it wasn't. I had permission to use it in a pinch just so long as I could get away with it. If I really messed up, it was whatever the judge said for impersonating an officer, because then they never heard of me in the Office of the Director, or—for that matter—across the river where Morley hung out.

"You been here long?" I asked.

"Eight years."

"Billie here all that time?"

"Yes."

"Pretty good friends?"

"I'd say so …"

"Okay," I said. "Now, listen hard. In all that time did Billie ever mention some people called the Marshalls?"

"The Marshalls?" She spelled it out.

"That's right," I said. "They had a ranch in the hills west of Easter back in the twenties, early thirties. William and Sarah Marshall and a boy named Davis Marshall. Did Billie ever mention them?"

Real Love Adventure shook her head. "No."

"You're sure about that?"

"Yes. There are only certain people she talks about. I know all their names and none of them are called Marshall."

"This Billie," I said. I tapped my temple. "How is she? Is she with it?"

The question didn't sit with her too well.

"Listen," I told her. "I'm *trying* to save the old biddy's life. Now, answer my question. Did she have all her marbles?"

"At times ..."

"How about this time?"

"She was fine," Real Love Adventure said. "She has good days and bad days. Today she was quite lucid. I'd say she was all right today."

Quite lucid. All right.

No, I told myself. If she is lucid today, she's not all right. If she's lucid, she is dead.

A deputy was waiting for me as arranged on the outskirts of Valentine. He was a youngster, he was much too cocky, and he had a lot of questions—like what was I doing with Lattimore's car, and where in the hell was Lattimore, and wasn't that blood soaking through the arm of the denim jacket? Cocky but not too observant. He didn't notice I had ripped away the patch with the stenciled name. Didn't notice because I kept my arm up covering the spot. Show 'em a little blood, maybe, but don't show 'em a ripped-away name patch, because then you've got problems. My own jacket was shoved under the front seat. It was really soaked in blood.

"I don't know," the deputy said.

I passed him the card that had convinced Real Love Adventure. "Now you do," I said. "So now move your ass. Fast."

We were about five miles the other side of Valentine when the call came in over the radio. The blue Dodge had elected to go through the roadblock. It had made it through but it hadn't made it much further. The driver had lost control and he had gone off the highway and down into a deep gorge. It was a mess and they didn't know yet about survivors.

The deputy was young and cocky and not too observant but he knew how to drive. We were about fifteen miles away from the crash scene when the call came and we got there in under ten minutes. I had a hard time keeping up.

By that time an ambulance had come down from Van Horn. The driver of the Dodge had been brought up from the gorge on a stretcher. He had a blanket over him and it had been pulled up all the way.

They were still struggling up the bank with Billie. I found the officer in charge, showed him the card saying I was FBI, and told him it was important—damn important—that I be allowed to talk to Billie.

He ran cold black eyes over me. "We'll see."

The ambulance attendants finally got her up on the roadside. She was an old lady and she was all smashed up and she didn't have very long anyway. The boss man nodded his permission. I leaned down beside her.

"Billie," I said. "I'm a police officer. Can you hear me?"

She made a gurgling sound. It wasn't a word. Just a sound.

"Billie," I said. "Listen carefully. What do you know about Davis Marshall?"

There were some more gurgling sounds. "I'm dying," Billie whispered.

"Please," I said.

"Beautiful," Billie whispered. "Simply beautiful…"

"Billie," I pleaded. "Listen to me. I'm a police officer and this is important."

The ambulance attendant at her side regarded me distastefully. "She's dead."

I checked for myself. There was no pulse. No heartbeat. No breath.

"Okay," I said. I walked over to the other stretcher and pulled back the blanket.

He was a tall man, getting on in years, and he wore glasses. Bits of plastic from the frames were imbedded in the flesh under his eyes. He had dark hair, sort of brownish, thinning a bit, and parted in the middle. Real Love Adventure disappointed me. She had missed the part in the middle.

He was not what you would call handsome. His nose was too long and the eyes were sort of squinty. There was a small but noticeable scar on the side of his mouth. His teeth were store-bought.

"Do you know this character?" the boss man asked.

"No," I said. I pulled the blanket back up. It was another disappointment. I had been looking forward to going fishing with Ace King.

The boss man got really nosey then. He asked the same questions as the cocky deputy plus one more. Why was the name tag torn off the jacket?

"I think we better have a little talk," I said.

"I think so, too," he said.

I got into his cruiser and he drove me to his office in Van Horn. I gave him a Washington number and he put in the call and a few minutes later he didn't have any more questions. He just did what he was told.

The service was pretty good. He had hamburgers and french fries and lots of hot coffee brought in from a cafe around the corner. He had a doctor pay a house call to pick three pieces of shrapnel out of me, two from my left arm, one from high up on the shoulder. He had the cocky deputy go out and buy me a new shirt and sports jacket, and the deputy, to my surprise, showed considerable good taste.

I was feeling pretty chipper again when I put in my call to Morley. The feeling didn't last long.

"Jesus Christ," Morley said after I had told him the story. It was the first time I had ever heard him take the name of our Lord in vain.

I didn't say anything.

"Three corpses," Morley said. "Three corpses and a police officer tied up in a pantry. Did you ever think of retiring?"

I thought of Lisa. "I can't," I said. "I'm in too deep."

There was a pause. He was lighting a cigarette. Oh, he was back on the weed, all right, and it was my fault.

"I had a man pay a call this morning on Marshall," Morley said. "It was an official call. The man explained the need for a very thorough background check on anybody who is thinking of running for President. Marshall said he was in complete agreement and he was most co-operative."

"Oh?"

"Most co-operative," Morley said. "He told us about his early childhood, how he lost both parents in a flu epidemic in thirty-six, and how he then went to live with friends of the family in El Paso."

"That's nice," I said. "Only it is too bad said friends are dead, huh?"

"On the contrary," Morley replied smoothly. "They now live in New York. The name is Sutton. Mr. and Mrs. Willard P. Sutton. Are you familiar with the Suttons?"

"I don't think so."

"Mr. Sutton is chairman of the board of Oil America. He is a director and major stockholder in about a dozen leading corporations across the country. I have the list here before me. Shall I read it?"

"No."

"Marshall went to school in El Paso while living with the Suttons," Morley continued. "That's in the records there. He finished grade ten. He dropped out, it seems, because he was behind a couple of years, and big for his age anyway. He went to work for Sutton. Banged around in Sutton's oil fields until Pearl Harbor. Then he joined the Army."

"Claiming a high school education," I pointed out.

"So he lied a little," Morley said. "Can you blame him? That would have quite a bearing on the kind of assignment he got in the Army. And you must admit he did very well from then on."

"I admit it."

"It's all coming in now," Morley said. "Reports on interviews with his fellow students at school in El Paso. The neighbors of the Suttons. The men he worked with in the oil fields. He's clean as a whistle."

"Sure," I said. "You want to know something? It would have been helpful if we'd had all this crap in his file in the first place."

"One of those things," Morley said. "Somebody got lazy and picked him up starting from the official records when he joined the Army. There really was no need to go back any further unless a serious question arose ...."

"How far back are you going?" I asked.

"We've gone all the way," Morley said. "Mr. Sutton first met the Marshall family in 1928. Davis Marshall was eight years old then. Sutton used to hunt that country and he got acquainted with the family when he asked permission to shoot on their property. He took a shine to the boy and when both parents died he took the lad in. No kids of his own."

"Why didn't he adopt him?"

"How should I know? Marshall was sixteen by that time. Maybe he didn't want to be adopted."

I thought for a moment. "Marshall's parents," I said. "Were they really married? Legally?"

Morley pulled on his cigarette. "No. That's the reason why Marshall has never said much publicly about his childhood."

"Fine," I said. "We've got a bastard running for President The fact that he is divorced isn't enough."

"The new morality," Morley said. He didn't sound concerned.

"I don't like it," I said. "I don't like any of it. How far are you going back on Sutton?"

"Four generations so far," Morley said. "The Suttons are more American than George Washington. They were in the paint business before they discovered oil. They invented colors ...."

"Red, white and blue."

"What's eating you?" Morley asked.

"Listen, sir," I said. "I don't care if Willard P. Sutton came over on the *Mayflower*. If Marshall is so clean, how come the moment I start asking questions around here all hell breaks loose, *sir*? Why the grenade in my lap? Why was Agnes bumped off? Why was Billie kidnapped?"

"You finished?"

"No," I said. "Ace King was some sort of Ruskie. He lived in Alamos and that means he was tied in with Jegalova. The Ruskies have got something on Marshall. They *want* him to be President. They are bumping off all the presidential candidates except one—Marshall."

"Now are you finished?"

"No," I said. "The Ruskies have something on Marshall. Whatever it is, it's so bad, so terrible, they think they can use it to blackmail him, twist him to their own ends. If we find out what that something is, the game is over, and that's why Ace King killed Agnes and kidnapped Billie, and that's why I'm hanging around here until I know everything there is to know about Davis Berwick Marshall."

"The *something* that interests you so much," Morley said. "Did it ever occur to you that it is connected in some way with Lisa? Did it ever enter your thick skull that the answer lies with the darling girl who had an abortion and then miraculously turned up as a virgin?"

That hurt. That really hurt. "That's why I'm not hanging around here," I said. "That's why I'm letting others find out everything there is to know about Davis Berwick Marshall. That's why I'm going back to Alamos. Now."

"Thank you," Morley said.

I was going to hang up. Then a question occurred to me. "I have a question," I said. "What if I can't find out what it is the Ruskies have on Marshall? What if no one can?"

"That's simple. I'll just have to ask him not to run for the presidency."

"One more question. What if Marshall tells you to go to hell?"

"That's simple, too," Morley said. "You'll just have to kill the stubborn son of a bitch."

"Very funny."

"Is it?" Morley asked. He hung up.

CHAPTER NINE

Hobart was asleep in my bunk in the caravan. He hadn't bothered to undress or even take off his boots. The cans from two six-packs of beer were scattered on the floor beside the bunk. Every one of them was empty.

"Sleeping beauty," I said. "Up and out of the sack. The day shift is here."

Hobart opened one eye. He regarded me sourly. He regarded his watch even more sourly. "That was fast."

"That's me," I said. "I'm quick. Speedy Sparrow. Now, out of the sack."

He sat up slowly. "How did you manage it?"

"U-Drive to El Paso," I said. "Then taxi across the border. Then I got smart. I climbed into the back seat of the taxi and had him drive me all the damn way to Chihuahua. By that time my pilot had flown down from Ojinaga. Hence by plane from Chihuahua to Alamos."

"Smart," Hobart said. "I figured you'd fly commercial from El Paso to Phoenix and then take an Aeronaves flight down to Ciudad Obregón. I wasn't expecting you back until about noon."

"Smart," I agreed. "I'm four hours early. The world owes me four hours and I'm going to spend them in that bunk."

"You slept in the taxi?"

"Four hours," I said. "Four plus four equals eight. A growing boy needs eight. So move it, huh?"

Hobart smiled. "Tough guy."

"You're damn right," I said. "You've heard about Morley's final solution? How tough can a guy get?"

I had gone through the long warm-up and now that was the pitch. I pretended to look away but I was watching carefully for his reaction.

He was immediately serious. "I doubt it will come to that ...."

The softly spoken words twisted into my stomach. I turned and stood staring at him in disbelief. How the hell could they be serious?

"Thanks," I said. "I notice you just have your doubts. You admit the possibility is there?"

He didn't answer.

"Supposing you were a presidential candidate and Morley asked you not to run?"

There was still no answer.

I kicked at the empty beer cans. "While we're at it, how come you're so damned relaxed, Hobart? A couple of days ago you were on the wagon. Now you're back swilling it like a pig."

"Two of them are mine, kid," he said easily. "I had some of the boys over last night. We had a long chat and the most anybody had was a couple of lousy beers. You mind?"

"Then what are they all doing piled up here?"

"I'm protecting my image."

I laughed. It made me feel a lot better.

"We're in pretty good shape," Hobart said. "Marshall started getting official protection as of yesterday morning. We've got more people guarding him than the Secret Service has on the President. The town is full of agents."

"What about Georgi boy?"

"He's covered."

"When do you pick him up?"

"When we've got a few more answers."

"Do you think he suspects we're on to him?"

"No. Why should he? And if he did, he wouldn't be hanging around, that's for damn sure."

I wasn't so damn sure. "What if Georgi sent Ace King after me? I come back. Ace doesn't. Georgi starts wondering what happened. Did Ace get caught and talk?"

"No," Hobart said. He finally relinquished the bunk. He got up, crossed to the sink, splashed some water in his face, and put on the coffee.

"Then what?" I asked.

"Ace was in a bind," Hobart said. "He had to act on his own. First, he sees you at four o'clock in the morning in Alamos. You say you're going to bed. Then he drives into Navojoa with Dutch to go fishing at the beach and who does he spot driving into the airport? You."

"So?"

"So this makes him suspicious. He knows how close you are getting to Marshall. He figures he better check out your sudden change of plans. So he ditches Dutch, goes back to the airport, starts asking questions. Your pilot didn't file a flight plan but he did mention he was going to Ojinaga. That means Easter."

"He hired a plane and took off after me?"

"That's right. And aren't we lucky that there are phones only at the hotels in Alamos? There was no way for Ace to get word to Georgi...."

"Providing Dutch is okay."

"Dutch is fine," Hobart said. "He was cheesed off when Ace ditched him but he went fishing anyway. Spent the whole day on the saltchuck. We picked him up coming in and he went along with us. The story is that it was rough out there and the boat got swamped and we lost poor old Ace King. Dutch is so broken up he's gone back home to San Diego."

"A likely story."

"Can you think of a better one?"

"Not at the moment," I admitted.

"Then can it," Hobart said. "If you had stayed put, I wouldn't have to tell these terrible lies, you know that? Think of all the money being wasted on the air-sea search."

I flaked out exhausted. I hadn't slept that well during the four-hour taxi ride from El Paso to Chihuahua. I kept waking up from dreams in which I had killed Davis Marshall.

"This protection," I said. "As soon as Marshall makes his candidacy official, then it's the normal routine, right? We bow out quietly and the Secret Service takes over ... ?"

"Of course."

I thought about that a while. "Doesn't that sort of complicate Morley's final solution?"

"It's not going to come to that," Hobart said.

"I know. But if it *does* ... ?"

Hobart sighed. "Don't you know why Morley chose you?"

"Sure," I said. "Because he hates me."

"Only partly." Hobart grinned. "The main reason is that if it must be done, you'll be in the best position, kid. You'll be an inside man—on his staff."

"*If* he asks me to join his staff."

"And *if* you accept when he asks."

I closed my eyes.

"You don't have to accept," Hobart said. "You can bow out now. Or you can fix it so you won't be asked."

"Bow out? Christ, the Russians are reaching for the presidency of the United States, and I can bow out, huh?"

"One of the last freedoms we all enjoy. Everybody still has the right to say no."

"Sure. But if it needs doing, really needs doing, and I won't do it, then Morley gets somebody else who will, right? What's the difference?"

"There isn't any difference," Hobart said. "No difference at all. So why don't you stop bellyaching?"

I didn't have any answer for that. I just lay there with my eyes closed and smelling the coffee as it started to perk. After a while Hobart brought a cup of it over to me. "What's really bugging you?" he asked.

"Lisa," I told him. "I have a fairly fertile and devious mind. I can imagine a lot of funny things happening on the way to the White House. Tell me, for example, that Stalin really didn't die, but that he is alive and living here in Alamos, disguised as Davis Marshall. Tell me that and I will say it is possible. Improbable, perhaps, but nevertheless possible, because plastic surgeons are real whizzes these days, and maybe they've found out a way to graft fingerprints."

Hobart laughed. "There's your answer. They grafted back her virginity."

I sat up. I wasn't joking any longer. "I'm willing to believe *that*," I said.

"So was Morley," Hobart said. "That's one of the many things I still have to tell you. We arranged for a slight accident yesterday afternoon for Lisa. This guy bumped into her car. She was all right, it seemed, but as soon as she got out to inspect the damage and this guy touched her, just put his hand on her arm, she collapsed in a heap."

"Oh?"

"That's right," Hobart said. "Luckily, there was this big house trailer right behind, and who should be driving it but an American doctor, just passing through on his vacation. Well, they carried the poor girl into the trailer, and since the doc wanted to find out what was wrong, he did have to examine her."

"And?"

Hobart smiled. "That thin and essentially ridiculous hunk of mucous membrane that usually covers part of the opening of the vagina in a virgin had been only recently busted. Bird name of Sparrow is the prime suspect."

"It wasn't a graft job?"

"It decidedly was not."

"She didn't fool me with a rubber band and ketchup?"

"No. You were the first, Charlie."

I blew on my coffee and took a sip. It was too hot and it was also too strong. "You've been a busy boy."

"Haven't I?" Hobart said. He had half of his coffee finished. Now he drained the rest in one gulp. He got up from his chair and went back for more.

I waited until he got back. "Twins," I said then. "Morley has been laughing at me but he's got to accept that explanation now. One person can't look just like another unless they are identical twins."

"Keerect," Hobart said.

That surprised me a little. "Then Morley does agree that we are dealing with identical twins?"

"Of course. What other possible explanation is there? Morley was waiting, naturally, for the results of yesterday's *accident,* but now that the virginity bit is confirmed—well, what other possible explanation is there, for Christ's sake?"

I slammed my coffee cup down. "That dirty bastard! You mean he's been giving me a hard time and all along he agreed it had to be twins?"

"Yes."

"Why?"

"Why accept your first and rather obvious conclusion?" Hobart grinned. "If your first explanation was accepted, you wouldn't try to come up with others, now would you? You'd get lazy and stop thinking..."

"The dirty bastard."

"I agree," Hobart said. "I agree with you wholeheartedly. Now, do you want to hear the rest?"

"Sure."

"Okay. The doctor who attended at Lisa's birth has been questioned. He is a very prominent physician and he states there was just the one child—not two. The nurse who attended with him, who is no longer associated with him, and who hasn't even seen him in ten years, has also been located and questioned. She states there was just the one child—not two."

"A conspiracy..."

"Certainly," Hobart said. "Now, would you like to know what happened last night in Philadelphia?"

"I don't think so."

"Last night in Philadelphia," Hobart said, "Dr. Raymond Marks, the personal physician of Mrs. Arago Sanvitores, the former Mrs. Davis Marshall, the mother of Lisa, you know?—this Dr. Marks just happened to call by the home of Mrs. Sanvitores. He was in the neighborhood and he just dropped by to say hello."

"Another of Morley's coincidences?"

"Yes."

"And?"

"As luck would have it, Mrs. Sanvitores chose that moment to have a slight stroke, or at least what looked like a stroke, and naturally the doctor had her rushed right over to his clinic. There, under the effects of Mytavol, more commonly known as a truth serum, Morley himself personally questioned the former Mrs. Davis Marshall. She stated, while in this hypnotic trance, that she just had the one child—not two."

"She did, huh?"

"She did," Hobart said. He passed me a note. "Now, why don't you get some sleep? It looks like you're going to need it."

The note was dated that morning and it smelled of perfume. It said:

Dear Charlie,

How could you run away on me like that? Yesterday was the longest day in my life. Tyler says you are supposed to be back by this afternoon. Therefore you are expected at four o'clock at the Casa Alegre. What we are going to do is, we are going to get slightly smashed, and then we are going to sneak off somewhere, and we are going to play that new game you taught me, right? Right.

Expectantly (not really, I hope),

Lisa.

"Christ," I said.

Hobart grinned. "Sleep."

"This handwriting," I said. "How does it compare with that of the girl who has been around the block so often?"

"It's the same," he answered. "Frankel is here. He's an expert and he checked it. He says it is the same handwriting."

Oh, sure, Hobart. Sleep. Wonderful sleep. The stuff of dreams.

Marshall himself met me at the door of the Casa Alegre. He gave me the old two-hander, one shaking, the other hugging. He seemed even more pleased than usual to see me. "Lisa is still fixing herself up," he grinned. "She'll be with you in a while. But not before she looks her best."

I grinned back at him. "She can't look any better."

"Wait and see," he said. "She's been positively radiant the past two days. What have you been doing to her?"

I was glad he didn't wait for an answer to that question.

"Come on," he said. "We've got time for a drink. There are a few things we need to talk over."

He led the way across the courtyard to his den. There was an old friend of mine sunning himself in a basket chair at the edge of the swimming pool. There had been another old friend sitting in a car parked outside.

"Who are all the strangers?" I asked when the den door closed behind me.

"Bodyguards," Marshall said. "They came on yesterday morning. I am now officially a ward of the United States Government."

I raised an eyebrow. "Even before you officially announce your candidacy?"

Marshall shrugged. "They think it is necessary. What will you have?"

"It's a little early. You having something?"

"I am."

"A martini, then."

He opened the doors of a portable bar and took out a bottle of Beefeater's. "How did the discussions go with your agent?"

"Fine," I said. Tyler had told Lisa that I had received a hurry-up call from my agent in Los Angeles. It looked as if I had a sale, the message went, but in order to sew it up, I had to meet with the publishers, work out a few things that were bugging them about the first half of the manuscript and how it was all going to be resolved in the end.

"Is it sold?"

I nodded. "I think so. All I have to do is keep up the pace. Why the frown?"

It vanished immediately. "Silly of me," he said. "I just can't help feeling disappointed. Here I was planning on how I was going to use all my influence to get it published and you go make a sale when it's not even completed . . . ."

"Your interest has been a big help," I said.

He grinned. "It's a damn fine book. You have my sincere congratulations."

"Thanks," I said. "I don't know whether I should congratulate you. The palace guard out there—you are really going to do it?"

"It seems my mind has been made up for me, doesn't it?"

"Not really. Tell them to go home. I'll write the announcement for you. 'Despite the urging of . . .' "

"No," he said firmly. "I told you before. I made the decision before any of this happened. I'm going to formally declare my candidacy just as soon as I get back to New York."

"That could be like signing your death warrant."

"I know that," he said. He did the bit with the shaker and poured out two martinis. I took one and we raised our glasses in a toast. Neither of us said anything as the glasses touched.

"I think I can tell you this," he said then.

"What's that?"

He eased himself into a chair by the fireplace. "I had a visitor early yesterday. Fellow from an intelligence agency I didn't even know existed. CI-2. You ever hear of it?"

"Read of it. But I didn't think they paid calls on people . . . ."

"He was for real, all right," Marshall said. "Two Secret Service agents were with him."

"The guards?"

"No. That's what I was going to tell you. Under the present law, even as recently amended by Congress, the Secret Service can't protect a presidential candidate until he formally declares, and the FBI really doesn't have jurisdiction. So to fill in the gap all probable candidates of any significance are now being protected by this CI-2."

"Better late than never?"

Marshall shrugged. "What do you expect? Hell, if they had moved any faster, they'd be protecting every Tom, Dick and Harry in the country. They had to wait until the situation sorted out a bit—to determine exactly who were the most likely candidates, and, more importantly, if they were *legitimate* candidates, with any hope at all in the primaries."

"And you are now considered a part of this group?"

"By default, mainly, I admit," he said. "I wouldn't be much of a contender at the moment if it hadn't been for this terrible series of assassinations. As you say, all a man of any standing has to do these days is suggest he would like to be President, and bang—he's dead."

"So why do it?"

Marshall considered for a moment. "This is a time of great crisis for our country," he said slowly. "We are obviously faced with some sort of enormous conspiracy. The killings of the last few months are plainly designed to create a vacuum—if not to leave the country leaderless, then to create a situation, impossible as it seems, where our enemies might be able to push forward their own choice as President."

I nodded and sipped at my drink.

"This is why I've been under such tremendous pressure to run from so many sectors," he said. "Not only from the business community, but from the conservative element as a whole, which regards me, I suppose, as their finest example of the Horatio Alger rags-to-riches hero in all America. I'm Mr. Free Enterprise."

I still didn't interrupt.

"I also enjoy, as you know, wide respect and perhaps even admiration in academic circles, thanks to my various philan-thropic gestures over the years, and I'm certainly not unaccept-able to the liberals and the civil rights groups."

"You haven't mentioned the party itself...."

"No," Marshall admitted. "The party doesn't really know which way to turn. Cannon, of course, was their obvious choice, a sure winner, and when he was killed—well, the party still hasn't recovered, that's all."

"Which is why you have to go the primary route?"

"Yes. I may be a national figure in my own right but I'm still *only* a businessman and I've never held any public office of par-ticular note. My four years as a state senator didn't prove any-thing. I haven't got a chance for the nomination unless I can go before the convention as a proven vote-getter on the national level. They'll just pull some senator out of the hat at the last moment and that will be that."

"Why not let them do it?"

"Why not?" Marshall mused. "I've also given that aspect of it considerable thought. But will the backroom choice be the man this country really needs at this time in our history ... ?" He leaned back solemnly in his chair. "I have my limitations, I know, but I think I am equipped—as well as any man—to be President, and perhaps much more equal to the task than the man who will emerge from the doubt, fear and compromise of the back room."

He had a pretty good point there. The doubt, fear and compromise could produce a really lousy choice in what was indeed a time of crisis. The President was seriously ill and couldn't possibly run for another term. The Vice-President had lost the respect and confidence of the country and couldn't be elected dogcatcher. Those who were coming forward to offer themselves as alternatives were being disposed of with a nightmarish professional skill ....

"You know my greatest fear?" he asked.

I shook my head.

"My greatest fear is that man will be a coward," he said. "If he waits until the last possible minute and then steps forward, that may mean that he was afraid of running in the primaries, fearful of his life. We can't afford that type of man as President. Today, of all times, we need a fearless man, a soldier. One who is willing to lay his life on the line right from the start."

"You just ruined a great idea of mine," I said. "This election, considering the danger to the candidates, I was thinking they should do away with the primaries entirely, and simply leave it up to the conventions. That way we'd at least have a few months free of all this killing."

"No," Marshall said firmly. "In the first place, Congress would never outlaw the primaries, and in the second, we'd be surrendering to the forces working against us—giving up one of our most cherished democratic rights. And what would be the next step? Outlaw all campaigning in public? Keep the candidates locked up somewhere until election day and permit them to campaign only on television and radio?"

"Perhaps that will be necessary ...."

"If it is, it will be a sad day for our country, my boy," Marshall said. "Then we might as well go all the way. Keep the President locked up for his whole four-year term. Never let him appear in public. Just allow in a few trusted advisors. If you find any advisors he will trust…"

The door to the adjoining bedroom had been partially open. Now it pushed out to reveal Lisa. "You two," she said. "You should hear the two of you. What a positively morbid conversation."

We both stood to greet her.

"Perhaps," Marshall said. "But it was all leading up to something I was hoping might make us all very happy. I was just about to ask this young man if he would consider joining my staff in my campaign for the presidency."

I looked at Lisa. I had expected to find some sort of answer in the marvelously deep green eyes. Oh, yes. No. Wait Something.

"Well?" Marshall asked.

Radiant, he had said, and she really was, damn it. Exquisite, sexy, quick and radiant. Positively radiant, and what have you been doing to her, anyway, Charlie?

"I'd be honored," I said. I stepped forward and took the outstretched hand.

"Done!" Marshall said.

Yes, I thought. I had done it, hadn't I? One of the last freedoms we all enjoy is the right to say no. But I hadn't exercised it and so now I was on his staff—an inside man. *The* inside man.

Oh, you're so God damn smart, Morley, and how's by you, Georgi N. Jegalova?

"I guess this calls for a celebration," Lisa said.

CHAPTER TEN

It was quite a celebration. It was almost two o'clock in the morning when I finally kissed Lisa good night at the door of the Casa Alegre. I'd again had too much to drink, but I was carrying it very well for a change, and as I crossed the cobblestones to my waiting caravan, I told myself that congratulations were very much in order for Charlie Sparrow.

I had done my duty. I had been taken on as a leading member of the campaign staff of Davis Berwick Marshall. I was, according to our understanding, going to be his chief speech writer during the campaign, and—barring unforeseen circumstances—I would be appointed press secretary if Marshall was elected President.

I smiled and recalled Morley's final words as he sent me away on what he had laughingly called Operation Alamos. "It's only temporary, you understand?" Morley had said. "If Marshall does run for the presidency, I want you right at his side, his personal bodyguard. If he makes it and offers you a permanent job, you can take that, too, but only on a temporary basis, you understand. You'll have to resign after a decent period...."

A decent period? I wondered how long that might be. Morley would dearly love a pipeline directly into the White House. That, I imagined, would be almost as good as having one into the Kremlin, and the revelations no doubt would be just as startling. But how long dare he keep it up? What was a decent period?

Perhaps—just perhaps—Morley could justify my presence as a member of Marshall's campaign staff. But the moment Marshall entered the White House it was an entirely different matter. My idea of a decent period, unless there were extenuating circumstances, a clear indication that the nation was in the direst danger, was about one second after Marshall took the oath of allegiance. One second, and then okay, mister, it is all yours, and may you walk with the Lord.

No. That wasn't right, I decided. The time to quit was right after the convention. I should carry him that far, protect him until he got the nomination, and then walk away from it. From that moment on no intelligence agency had any damn business having an agent in a policy-making role on a presidential candidate's staff.

That, at any rate, was my idea, and perhaps it was Morley's idea, too. You never knew what he was really thinking. You could only guess as to what were his actual intentions. The idea of me going right into the White House—that might be just crap, making the assignment sound more important and exciting than it really was, a way of guaranteeing my acceptance. And the thought that he might resort to ordering the death of Marshall—Christ, that was really crazy, a means of testing my faith and loyalty, wasn't it?

Morley. You never knew Morley. Always so cool and smart …

I turned back and faced the Casa Alegre. Lisa's good night kiss was still warm on my lips. If you are so God damn smart, Morley, will you hurry up, please, and explain why that girl is that kind of girl? Will you do that for me? *Please?*

"You ever going home?"

I swung around slowly. H. H. Goding, alias Georgi N. Jegalova, was sitting in the cab of my truck, wiping the sleep from his eyes. He apparently had been flaked out on the seat waiting for me.

"Good morning," I said. "What in the hell are you doing out at this time of night? Looking for broads … ?"

"I have a problem," H. H. Goding told me. "Get in and drive me home. I shall attempt to discuss it with you."

"All right," I said. I went around the truck. The palace guard posted in the car parked in front of the Casa Alegre watched me with what appeared to be complete disinterest. He would be aware, of course, that H. H. Goding wasn't H. H. Goding, but he hadn't called me over when I left the casa. He hadn't warned me of who was waiting. And where the hell was the constant surveillance?

H. H. Goding grinned as I clambered behind the wheel. "I guess I was wrong," he said.

"Oh?"

"That Lisa," he said. "You must be really making out. I thought for a while that you intended to stay for the night."

I offered him a Viceroy. He declined and I lit it for myself. "I appreciate your interest," I said. "Up to a point." I blew out the smoke. "That point has just been passed."

He laughed easily. "You want to travel light, huh? First you dump Maggie. Now me...."

"Don't be ridiculous," I told him. "I'm not dumping anyone. You've got to be aboard before you can be dumped. Maggie was never aboard."

"Nor me?"

I turned to look at him. "Listen," I said. "I like you. We've had some good talks together. But I've only known you for a couple of weeks, old man, and that hardly makes you my bosom buddy, now does it?"

He stared back at me. "How long have you known Lisa?"

"Jesus," I said. "You are starting to get out of hand. Do you know that? You are really starting..."

"All right," he said amiably. "I am an old man and I am out of hand. That is my problem. Now, drive me home."

I turned on the ignition. The palace guard was still sitting in his car. He watched with the same apparent lack of interest as we drove past him and rounded the block. There was no sign of any other surveillance.

"I take it Marshall has decided to run," H. H. Goding said. It wasn't a question.

"Oh?"

"Don't shit the troops," he said. "I may be old but I am not blind. That is a cop parked at the front door."

"Did he check you?"

"Of course. He wanted to know what I was doing getting into your truck. I had to tell him my name and show him my identification. He checked me off against a list he's got in the car."

"Oh?"

"You keep saying *oh*. But that's a cop, Charlie, and he's got a master list of everyone in town, and he is being extremely careful of anybody who comes within spitting distance of the Casa Alegre. Which means that Marshall has decided he is going to run for President."

"Oh," I said.

H. H. Goding laughed his easy laugh. "It must be exciting for you. I've been watching Marshall, and he really likes you, Charlie. He likes you a lot. He also thinks you're a great writer. I wouldn't be surprised if he offered you a job...."

"Really?"

"Really," he said. He regarded me thoughtfully. "Has he?"

I mulled that one over. I told myself to put aside all knowledge that this was Georgi N. Jegalova. As far as I knew, I told myself, he was H. H. Goding, an old man, a hanger-on, a casual acquaintance of a couple three weeks standing. Under those circumstances, was there any reason why I, the writer fellow, the slightly hip young man in the way-out caravan, should confide in H. H. Goding?

"Well...?"

"That's hardly any business of yours," I told him.

He sighed. "It was ever thus. I've been living in this sleepy little dump for almost twenty years. *Finally* something happens. We've got a presidential candidate right in our midst and I know his daughter's boyfriend. But will he tell me what is going on? Will he let me in on any of the juicy details? No ...."

I didn't answer him. I tried to put myself in his place. There was no reason why I should suspect he was other than H. H. Goding. Despite our so recent acquaintance, we got along very well, and we had had some good talks together, hadn't we? And so what was wrong in him playing a silly old man all excited about having a presidential candidate in town? What was suspicious about him asking me to confirm the fact that Marshall had decided to run?

Now there was an edge of complaint in his voice. "Suddenly he clams up ...."

I smiled at him. Was this what he wanted from me? Confirmation of the fact that Marshall definitely had decided to run for President? And what would happen if this was confirmed for him? Would the assassins move again?

"My old buddy," H. H. Goding complained. "Yesterday we were friends. Today he doesn't know me ...."

If it was confirmation he wanted, he wanted it damn badly, didn't he? He must want it something terrible if he was waiting in the cab of my truck at two o'clock in the morning.

"You said you had a problem," I reminded him.

He turned away as if embarrassed. "Forget it."

"No," I said. "If it's important enough for you to lose your sleep over it, I want to hear about it, old man."

"Oh?"

"That's my line."

"Well," H. H. Goding said. He turned back to me and ran a worn finger under his nose. "To be quite truthful, I'm in a real bind, Charlie."

"What kind of bind?"

"Financial. My check hasn't come this month and they're going to cut off my electricity tomorrow morning. There goes my water pump. There goes my freezer. There ..."

"My God," I said. "Why didn't you say something earlier?" I pulled out my wallet. "How much do you need? Will a hundred hold you?"

"Fifty," he said. "I hate to ask…"

I gave him five twenties. "Take the hundred. Just in case…."

"Thanks," he said. "The check ought to come any day. I'll pay you back just as soon as it comes."

"Anytime," I told him.

We rode in silence for the last couple of blocks to his house. He made no further attempt to pump me about Marshall. I wasn't about to volunteer anything.

He punched me on the arm as he got out of the cab. The same gesture of affection once favored by Ace King. "Thanks again."

"You're welcome."

"It's funny," he said, closing the door. "I must be getting proud or something. You're the only person in town I could bring myself to ask. The only one."

"Don't be silly," I told him. "You've got lots of good friends here. Dozens of them."

"Have I?" he asked. He thought for a moment. "Maybe. Maybe not. It's hard to tell sometimes…."

I watched him go into his house. He had a real spring in his step for a man of his age. But then he wasn't a man of his age. Nor was he broke.

"Good night," I called. If he answered, it was lost by the smack of the screen door, slamming closed behind him.

I drove to the highway and then circled back to within a couple of blocks of the miniature casa Tyler claimed to have rented from the Seven Dwarfs. I parked the caravan in a vacant lot hidden by crumbling walls and walked the rest of the way. The door was pulled open before I could knock.

"Enter," Hobart said. He led the way back to the pint-sized kitchen. Tyler was there listening to a squawk box.

"Shhhh," Tyler whispered.

I bent my head toward the box. The creak of footsteps, a door opening and closing, the rustle of clothing, a loud banging noise, and then the very distinct sounds of a toilet bowl being put to its primary use.

Tyler frowned and turned down the volume.

"Georgi?" I asked.

"Yeah," he managed.

Hobart poured me a cup of coffee and passed it over Tyler's head. I accepted it gratefully and sat down at the yard-square table. My heavy load of liquor was starting to catch up on me.

"What do you think?" Hobart asked.

"About what?"

Hobart pointed a thick finger to the squawk box. "The guy who owes you a hundred bucks..."

"Oh," I said. I blew on my coffee. "When did you rig the caravan?"

"While you were in Easter."

"I never noticed," I said. The coffee, as usual, was much too strong. Hobart's version of half-and-half. Half beans.

"You're getting sloppy, kid," Hobart said. He eased around Tyler and sat down next to me. "You're also starting to drink too much. You smell of bourbon. Expensive bourbon."

"Only the best," I told him. "It is eight thousand years old. Aged in oak flasks made from the wreckage of the Ark." I blew at him. "Nice, huh?"

He pretended to wipe spittle from the corner of his eye. "Now, let's start over. What do you think?"

"I think he tried to pump me," I said. "He tried to get me to confirm that Marshall is going to run for President...."

"And?"

"He wants to know badly. He couldn't wait until tomorrow...."

"And?"

"I handled him beautifully."

Hobart sighed and rubbed his eyes.

"Shhh," Tyler said. He turned up the volume on the squawk box. The gurgles of a toilet flushing were mixed with the splash of water in a basin. We waited for the bathroom door to open but it didn't. Instead, there was the sound of the shower being turned on. Tyler lowered the volume again.

"Damn it," Hobart said. He looked at his watch.

"What do *you* think?" I asked.

Hobart shook his bull head. "I don't know...."

"Surely he wouldn't try anything himself?"

"I don't know," Hobart repeated tiredly. "Nothing figures about this bastard. You talk about dedication. Christ, he's been living here for twenty years, barely making ends meet. Why choose a pauper's existence as a cover?"

I tried the coffee again. "Because it's the best."

"Sure," Hobart admitted. "But for twenty years? Considering his record of service, you'd think he'd demand something better than that, wouldn't you?"

"So what's Khrushchev got that's better? Georgi at least has a house. Old Khrush only has an apartment...."

Hobart rewarded me with a pained smile.

I gave up on the coffee. "How long do we play with him?"

"I don't know that either," Hobart confessed. "Morley's idea is to just keep watching him, hoping that he'll lead us to others, and that they will lead us to still others."

"A bird in the hand..."

"Makes picking the nose difficult," Hobart said. "Look at it this way, kid. If we pick him up—which, seeing as how this is Mexico, would be a bit dicey—what have we got? We've got an old man who is as tough as railroad spikes and who is not going to talk. He's not even going to tell us what year it is."

"Maybe."

"Maybe, shit," Hobart said. "I know the type. Anybody who can stick it out here for twenty years, not even owning a car, is dedicated, kid. We wouldn't get a word out of him. Not one."

I lit a Viceroy.

"This is a long shower," Tyler complained.

Hobart looked at his watch. "Four minutes...."

"Okay," I said. "But there are other ways of looking at it. Georgi was once very close to the top in the Soviet Union. He still may be right up there and he may be the big push behind the effort to wipe out every damn man with the faintest intention of running for President. Right now, standing in that shower, rubbing soap in his armpits, he may be plotting a way to bump off Marshall. How about that?"

"Marshall is covered," Hobart said.

I couldn't leave it alone. "What about the other candidates who are left? Wouldn't it be just great if Georgi is the man who decides who gets it and when they get it? We're just watching, and he's mixing with everybody in town, any one of whom may be his contact, and so what's to stop him from giving the word...?"

"Nothing," Hobart said. "But if we get rid of him, somebody else takes his place, right? So what's the difference? Better we should watch. If we are patient, we may get a break."

"I still say this is a long shower," Tyler muttered.

Hobart took another look at his watch. "Do we have a textbook somewhere on how long a guy should spend in a shower?"

"It's on the shelf there," I said. "It's disguised as a tin of asparagus soup. If you hold it up to the light..."

"Almost six minutes," Tyler said.

Hobart sucked at his teeth. "Out," he ordered.

The shower stopped abruptly. There was a sound of bare feet squeaking on wet tile, a towel flapping, little murmurs of pleasure.

Hobart smiled coyly. "Incidentally," he said. "What do you suggest as the grounds for arresting Georgi? That he's impersonating an American while living in Mexico?"

I gave up. "Okay," I said. "Watch him. Play with him forever. See if I give a damn."

The bathroom door opened and closed. Wet feet flapped down a corridor. Creak of bedsprings. Throat being cleared. Measured breathing...

"Why don't you go home?" Hobart asked.

I held up my half-smoked Viceroy.

Hobart shrugged and put his face in his hands.

I sat there listening to the steady rhythm of Georgi's breathing. He had the blood of millions on his hands and he could fall asleep like an innocent babe.

Tyler's eyes started to close.

Breath in. Breath out. Breath in. Breath...

"What's that little squeaking noise?" I asked.

Tyler opened one eye. "The bedsprings. He's got this chick in bed, see, and what he's doing is, he is..."

"What squeaking noise?" Hobart demanded. He turned up the volume to its highest pitch.

"That one," I said.

He listened for a moment. "What is it?"

"I'm not sure," I told him. "But I have a tape recorder that sounds just like it. One of the reels squeaks."

Hobart dragged a walkie-talkie out from under the table. "Raven," he said urgently. "This is Eagle. Over."

"Raven," a palace guard said. "I read you loud and clear. Over."

"The pig may be loose," Hobart said. "Watch for him. Over and out." He looked at me. "You sure?"

I nodded.

"Jesus," Hobart said. He spoke again into the walkie-talkie. "Hawk," he said. "This is Eagle. Did you hear that last transmission? Over."

"Hawk," a voice said. "I heard it. But I don't figure it. Over."

"Our squawker is squeaking. We may be listening to a tape. Are you sure the pig is there? Over."

"Not positive. All we know is he went in and he didn't come out. What are you suggesting? A secret exit? Over."

Hobart stared at me. I shrugged and put out my cigarette.

"Hawk," Hobart said. "Go to the pen. Knock on the door. Hammer on the son of a bitch. If the pig answers, tell him you are lost, and which way is the hotel. Over."

"Roger."

The three of us looked at our watches. It was almost half past two. If we had been listening to a tape, Georgi could be long gone, perhaps halfway to Navojoa, or maybe climbing over the wall into the Casa Alegre.

Hobart swore softly. "Twenty years. Long enough to dig a tunnel to Chihuahua."

"Or a simple passage to the ruins next-door," I said.

There was a banging noise on the squawk box. Hawk hammering at the front door. Loud enough to wake up someone down the block. The measured breathing continued. It didn't miss a beat.

Hobart waited for a few more precious seconds. "Okay," he told Tyler. "You stay here. I want somebody on every road. If he's running away, just tail him, no pickup. I also want everybody in the casa on top of Marshall. If Georgi shows, they don't take any chances, hear? They shoot to kill."

"Right," Tyler said. He reached for the walkie-talkie.

Hobart pulled his holster off the back of his chair and headed out the door. I hadn't been invited, and then I hadn't been asked to stay, either. I went after him.

He stopped me at his car. "No," he said. "If you show up at Marshall's, it's going to look strange, kid. I'm sorry—but no."

I couldn't argue with the sense of that. I stood aside helplessly as he lurched away on squealing tires. Georgi N. Jegalova, a man who had killed millions, was on the loose, and he might be headed for Marshall. For Marshall and for Lisa. Only I couldn't go to her side. That would look strange...

I lit another Viceroy. Think, I told myself. Think, think, think. You are Georgi N. Jegalova. You have chosen tonight to kill Davis Berwick Marshall. Yet you know that there are guards outside the Casa Alegre. You know they are outside and therefore they are probably inside. That makes it difficult for you. Very difficult for an old man. Unless...

I thought of the other assassinations. There was no pattern to them. A rifle. A bomb in a package. An airplane sabotaged. It didn't matter if people in addition to the intended victim died. They would slaughter all those around him if necessary to get at their man.

Distance. That's what you need, isn't it, Georgi? Distance. Distance from your target.

Distance solved the problem of the guards both outside and inside the Casa Alegre. Distance also provided you the time you needed to get back to your house and switch off the tape and replace that recorded breathing with your own measured intake and exhalation of the air that should have been denied you when the first drop of blood stained those well-manicured hands.

Distance.

I tossed away the cigarette and started running. Georgi would be there by now, I told myself, but he would have taken his time, darting from shadow to shadow, taking every precaution not to be seen, and so he wouldn't have been there very long. He'd also have to take the time to assemble the thing and so that would be a further delay. Assemble it, position it, load it, aim it...

Time.

I should have told Tyler. I should have gone back into the house first and told Tyler to clear everybody from the Casa Alegre. I should have done that, but my instinct was to start running, and until I got there I couldn't be sure that I was right. I could be wrong and if I was wrong and they cleared the Casa Alegre and Marshall came out into the open...

I slowed down. There was less than a block to go. Georgi might hear my footsteps if I continued to run. I moved into the shadow of a wall and walked quickly but carefully to the corner.

Perspiration started to chill on me. I pulled in my breath and peered around the wall. As I had hoped, the roof of the church, from this angle, blocked out the bell tower. That made it a lot easier. I slipped off my shoes and picked my way across the cobblestone street and up the steps to the side door of the church. I tugged at it gently. It was locked.

I tried to picture the church in my mind. If this side door was locked, surely the front doors were locked, and the door on the other side, too. It didn't make sense to lock one door and not another. But if Georgi had unlocked a door, perhaps he had left it ajar, because he would be in a damn big hurry on his way out....

The front doors? No, they were too much in the open, visible from all sides of the plaza. He would have used either a side door or have entered through the rectory at the rear. Providing that was the rectory. Did the priest live there? Or was it just a changing room?

I cursed myself for not being a Catholic. If I was, I might know, and if I knew, it might help. I decided to circle around back. First, the rear door, then the door on the far side, then the front doors facing the plaza. If they were all locked....

The lock on the rear door was a primitive arrangement and it was loose on the jamb. All I had to do was to lean on it and the whole casing pulled away. The only sound was the screws easing out of rotten wood.

I stepped inside, closed the door behind me, and flashed on my penlight. It wasn't a rectory. Just a storeroom. A place to change. I padded across it and parted the curtains on the far door. This provided a side view of the altar. I switched off the light and slipped past the curtains and stood waiting for my eyes to adjust to the darkness.

There was just enough moonlight filtering through the stained-glass windows. I picked my way across the altar, down the three short steps, and along to the end of the aisle. There was a door there to my right. It was standing open.

I stopped in the doorway. It was pitch-black and I didn't dare use my light. I inched forward with my foot, found a stair, located a handrail, and moved up stealthily, praying that none of the stairs would creak. Halfway up the circular staircase there was moonlight again. That meant the door at the top was open.

I stood for a moment and listened. There was no sound. Nothing. That could mean one of two things. Either he wasn't there. Or he was waiting for me.

I moved up two more steps and stopped again. This time there was a sound. A very faint brushing noise. Clothing against stone? I held my breath and a pigeon cooed.

The breath pushed out of me. He couldn't be in the tower. Not with a pigeon still there. I ran up the last few stairs and touched off a sudden clatter of wings. There must have been at least half a dozen of them. They seemed to take off in that many directions.

God damn it, I thought. I was relieved and yet disappointed. I had been so certain of finding him in the tower. It was the only logical place for him to be to get a clear shot. There was only one place higher than the church tower and that was the hill in the center of the town. But the jail was located on the hill. He wouldn't dare fire from there.

I brushed the bell rope aside and crossed carefully to the low railing. This only served to confirm my original thinking. There was an unobstructed view across several blocks into the court-yard of the Casa Alegre. It would be so easy. So incredibly easy. A rocket launcher set up in the tower could lob half a dozen high-explosive bombs into that perfect target at five-second intervals.

That's all it would take. Thirty seconds of bombardment. Thirty seconds and there would be no more Casa Alegre. No Marshall. No Lisa.

I looked up and found myself staring at the black hump of the Cerro de Guadalupe. No, I thought. No. Why did I dismiss all hills when I dismissed the hill with the jail on it? Why didn't I realize that he might go outside of town and climb up the Cerro de Guadalupe?

It was much further away, a tougher shot to make, but if he knew what he was doing—well, the result would be the same, that's all. A total wipe-out.

I swung around desperately. It was hard to tell who was the most surprised. Me or Georgi N. Jegalova.

He was surprised, no doubt about it, but he was also ready, because he had a big black automatic in his right hand. All he had to do was move it three inches. Then it was pointing straight at my heart.

We stood staring at each other in mutual disbelief. It was only for a moment but it was time enough for me to take it all in. I had been right all along. The pack on his back held a rocket launcher.

"So," Georgi said. The automatic steadied in his hand. It was the continuous-feed model and it had a silencer on the barrel. That meant every slug in it practically all at once and the only sound would be thud, thud, thud…

"You're too late," I said. "The house has been evacuated. Better luck next time."

He edged around me. "Back," he whispered. "Back, back…"

I knew he was going to fire. It showed very clearly in the pale blue eyes. He was going to pull the trigger just as soon as he had me away from the low railing. He was going to kill me the moment he was certain I would fall back down the steps instead of over the railing. If I fell over the railing, I would make a noise, bouncing off the roof, splattering on the concrete sidewalk.

I fell over the railing.

Georgi hadn't expected that. His mouth opened as if to cry out a warning. The bell swung into his face, the edge of it clipping him under the jaw, and he went over the railing in a perfect arc, the weight of the rocket launcher taking him. He made no sound until he hit the sidewalk.

I hadn't expected it either. I had grabbed at the bell rope as I fell, but it was only to try to save myself, not to get at Georgi. I saw it as a way of breaking my fall a portion of the way down. It wasn't long enough to do much good. It only reached to the floor of the tower. But there was a knot in the end and that was something. It would break my fall there, when my fist slid down to the knot, and then I might get a grip on the roughhewn rocks of the tower, and then...?

That, in the split second left to me, seemed the only solution, but it hadn't worked that way. Fear had taken over and my grip had been like death. I hadn't allowed my hand to slip down the rope to the knot. So the bell had gone whipping across the tower before Georgi had a chance to react. It had gone whipping across and it had struck him in the face and now he was gone. He had gone over the railing in a perfect arc. Two stocking feet hanging in space for an instant. Then nothing.

I swung back into the tower and grabbed the bell's clapper. It had been clanging like crazy and the whole town would be awake by now. If I hurried, I thought, I'd just have time to get away, to be out of the church before someone came to investigate.

I took the stairs three at a time. Morley was going to be mad as hell, I thought. The idea was to just keep watching him, hoping that he would lead us to others, and that they would lead us to still others. Now all hope of that was over the railing and splattered on the sidewalk. But that was hardly my fault.

If he says anything, you ought to have this really good comeback, I told myself. If Morley says anything, tell him, What are you bitching about, *sir?* I'm out a hundred bucks.

CHAPTER ELEVEN

"Okay," Morley said, biting down on his lower lip. "Let's not take all day about it. Try the next one."

Hobart dropped another shell into the rocket launcher. It went whooshing across the desert and exploded with a huge puff of smoke.

"I think that was it," Morley said. He turned impatiently to the sergeant. "Well? What was the reading on that one?"

The sergeant was an old tech and he was not impressed. He waved a hand for silence while he listened to the report on his field telephone.

Morley stared hatefully at him. "You'll see," he told me.

The sergeant put down the phone. "They didn't get a reading…"

"Thank you, sergeant," Morley said. He turned away abruptly and strode back to the Jeep. He didn't say another word until we had signed off the base and were headed back to Phoenix in his U-Drive Pontiac. Then it was only to complain about the arrangements for the test.

There was never any figuring him, I thought. He had proved his point and still he wasn't satisfied. But then perhaps he was never satisfied. I flicked my eyes at the rear-view mirror. It was amazing how little I knew about him.

I knew his name. I knew he was in his early fifties, that he was overweight, and that he wore conservative clothes a trifle too tight-fitting. He had essentially a woman's face, round, liberally sprinkled with freckles, and topped off with red hair—now turning gray—worn too long and too wavy. If he put a shawl over his head he could pass for a grandmother. He was married, or at least he wore a wedding ring, and he had indicated once, a mistake on his part, that he was dissatisfied with the arrangement.

"You want to stop somewhere for lunch?" I asked.

"No," Morley said. "I had a late breakfast."

Wonderful. I had missed breakfast. Now I was going to miss lunch. It was going on two o'clock and I was hungry. Damned hungry and damned tired.

Hobart gave voice to my complaint. "We didn't," he said.

Morley moved his briefcase in his lap. "This won't take long."

I wondered what was going on in the mass of nerve tissue in that red-thatched cranium. Morley's contention for the beginning had been that Georgi never intended to blow up the Casa Alegre. What Georgi planned to do, Morley had said, was to fake an assassination attempt against Marshall, so that people wouldn't start asking why Marshall was being spared while every other candidate was being blasted.

Our tests on Georgi's bombs seemed to confirm the theory. There were six of them and they all were different. One was powerful enough to level a house. That one, Morley figured, was designated to fall short, wiping out a neighbor's casa—not Marshall's. Then, as the gunner's aim improved, the bombs became less powerful, until the one that landed on the roof of Marshall's bedroom was all noise and smoke.

Complicated but cute. The Casa Alegre would look like a disaster area. One section of it, the servants quarters, or perhaps even the guest wing, would be in ruins, with people injured and maybe dying. There would be a small crater amid the ruins in the other half of the block. The house across the street would be badly damaged. The one down further on the corner would be leveled...

There would be only one comment when someone looked at that mess. Well, they tried to get Marshall, but he was luckier than hell, as usual.

Morley had been so quick and so sure in his contention that it had been planned as a fake assassination bid, it could mean only one thing, I thought. Morley knew something he still hadn't passed on. Some new information on Marshall.

I pushed a little harder with the Pontiac. The sooner we got back to the motel, the sooner he would tell us, the sooner we could eat.

Morley was looking very proud of himself. He snapped open his briefcase and drew out a number of papers and photographs. He spread them out on the coffee table in an overlapping pile for easy reference.

"Exhibit One," Morley said. He picked up the first piece of paper and handed it to me.

It was an FBI report that had been dated only two days earlier. The results of a background check on a Shirley Larson. That was her married name. Her father, Jules Rauschenbusch, had been born in Russia, immigrating to the United States in 1924. Her brother, Jules II, a schoolteacher, had attended the University of Pennsylvania and while there he had joined the Fabian-spawned Intercollegiate Socialist Society. Shirley in her student days had been a delegate to communist-sponsored youth conferences behind the Iron Curtain. Now she was a nurse.

"Exhibit Two," Morley said.

It was a CI-2 file, so new it hadn't even been dated (a process that would be accomplished once it was approved by Morley), on Dr. Nelles Wasserman, the prominent doctor who attended at the birth of Lisa Marshall. The file said there was nothing to indicate Wasserman had ever belonged to or been associated with left-wing, socialist or communist organizations. It added, however, that there was evidence indicating the good doctor would do almost anything for a price—the reason, probably, that he was so darn prominent. Two years after Lisa's birth, which took place at the doctor's clinic, Wasserman's wife sued for divorce, citing

Shirley Rauschenbusch as corespondent. The suit claimed their affair began in November of 1950.

There was an FBI file along with Exhibit Two. It also said there was nothing to indicate Wasserman had ever belonged to or been associated with left-wing, socialist or communist organizations, despite his long association with and employment of Shirley Rauschenbusch.

Exhibit Three was a photostat copy of a birth certificate showing that a Nada Yarmolinski had been born January 28, 1952, in the Russian embassy in Washington, D.C., to the wife of Third Undersecretary Boris Yarmolinski. Attached was a notation that Boris and Olga Yarmolinski left the United States in May of 1952.

Exhibit Four was a series of photographs with the little red dots along the right edge identifying them as being taken from a U-2. The first photograph showed a village in a mountain valley and covered an area of about ten square miles. Each succeeding photograph zoomed in closer on the village until the last one, grossly magnified, showed an area of only a few square yards, a small section of street in the village.

Morley pointed with a pencil tip. "What's that?"

"A Volkswagen," I said.

The pencil moved. "And this?"

"Hard to tell. It's a big bastard. A Cadillac?"

"Lincoln Continental," Morley said. The pencil moved again. "How about these doodads?"

They were just dots. "Give me a hint," I said.

Morley smiled at Hobart. "Have you got a nickel?"

"Parking meters," I said.

Morley shuffled all the U-2 photographs back together. "What was so strange about the first photograph?"

That was easy. "No roads into the village. No airstrip. No water access."

Exhibit Five was a CI-2 file, again undated, on a Twerter Lasky, who had worked for almost eighteen years as a nurse-maid-babysitter-governess-companion in the Marshall household. She had been absolutely devoted to Lisa. Practically worshiped the child. Kept albums full of pictures, had her first words on tape, reel after reel of home movies, even saved her old school scribblers, blah, blah, blah. Lisa returned the affection and had been very broken up when Twerter's death came shortly after Jay Edgar's. Twerter had been born in Hungary. She had many relatives there. The investigation into her background was continuing. An FBI report also was pending.

Exhibit Six was another series of photographs, most of them taken with a miniature camera, depicting various activities of a distinguished-looking officer in the MVD, Colonel Ragar Tukovik, who is rumored to be the head of the Kykov Institute. In one photograph he was at the wheel of a Lincoln Continental. In another he appeared to be at some sort of cocktail party. There was a young woman off to one side. She looked awfully familiar.

"It's all conjecture," Morley said.

"Yeah," I said. I sat staring at the pile of crap he had taken from his briefcase. Con.jec.ture (kon-jek'chēr), *n*. [<L. *con-jicere*, to guess]. 1. guesswork; inferring, theorizing, or predicting from incomplete evidence. 2. a guess.

I sat staring at the pile of crap and did my guesswork.

Twins. Identical twins. That was the only explanation, and the switch had to have been made after August 11, 1970, the day that Lisa Marshall, who could afford the very best, had her pregnancy aborted in the swank Park Avenue clinic of Dr. Benjamin Sparks, the sassiety gurl's li'l ol' fixer-upper. The Pill is great, but if you are on the booze besides being on your back, you can get sloppy and forget to take it for a few days, and then oops!—no period. Period means the end. No period means the beginning. You begin to worry and fret and fuss and fume. How could I have been so *stupid*? No period, Lisa, darling, means the beginning, an egg fertilized, starting to grow, increasing in size with each passing day. You've got two choices. Lay it. Or get rid of it.

Friday, August 11, 1970. The file showed she settled down after that. If she had any more affairs, she was very discreet about it, and she had the opportunity to be discreet, because she took to traveling then. Europe. Africa. The Far East. But mostly Europe. She liked Europe a whole lot, especially Paris, but then we all like Paris, don't we, Lisa? Paris in the springtime. The pretty flowers and the crusty bread. The slate rooftops and the red wine. The soft, soft rain, and the impossible treasures, and the sun busting through, and the checkered tablecloths, and the song in your heart—and the handsome, gallant, *discreet* men.

Friday. August 11, 1970. Any time after that. She went away as Lisa Marshall and she came back as Lisa Marshall but she wasn't Lisa Marshall. Somewhere along the line a switch had been made. One girl went in a door and another came out. The new girl, the substitute, looked almost identical, because she was, after all, the identical twin. That's the key word. *Almost* identical.

There are differences and parents and close friends can tell identical twins apart without looking twice. But supposing, just supposing, that the idea of an identical twin existing had never entered the minds of the parents and close friends, and supposing, just supposing, that the real Lisa Marshall went away to Europe on March 28 and that the substitute Lisa Marshall, the identical twin no one even conceived of existing, returned in her place on September 2.

The parents and close friends would notice a difference. There would be a lot of little things that would be different. My, what a difference in Lisa, they would say. Hasn't that girl changed? Five months in Europe and you wouldn't believe it was the same girl!

They might all say that but none of them would point an accusing finger and seriously charge that the girl standing before them was not in fact Lisa Marshall.

Or would they? Hell, a mother would *know*, wouldn't she? Or even a father? Wouldn't some basic instinct prevail? Wouldn't there be some flashing sign blinking the words at you? This ain't your darling daughter?

Perhaps. Perhaps not. The point, dear parents, is that even though you have really never seen this girl before in your lives, she looks the same, she acts the same, and she talks the same as your Lisa. Not only that, folks, and this is the hard part—she *is* your daughter.

Twins. Identical twins. That was the only explanation, and one had to be taken away at birth, January 27, 1952. Mrs. Davis Marshall was going to have twins, only she didn't know it, because her doctor hadn't told her. At the first hint of twins, the doctor had mentioned it to his nurse, who was also his mistress, and whose purpose in being his nurse and his mistress was to find out all she could about his prominent and influential patients.

The nurse reported to her superior. The superior had a bright idea. Yes, said the nurse, her eyes widening, and so it came about that the birth took place at the doctor's clinic, with just the doctor and the nurse in attendance.

Mrs. Marshall was out cold when the babies came. She didn't know how many babies she gave birth to that night. It could have been one, it could have been two, it could have been three. It could have been a two-headed jackass in purple underwear singing God Save America. How the hell could she know?

And Davis Marshall. That's him out in the waiting room. Walking in circles, drinking coffee, smoking cigarettes. What does he know? The nurse comes out. She has one, count 'em, one, little bundle of joy in that pink blanket, and she says, "Congratulations, Mr. Marshall. You've just become the proud father of a bouncing baby girl." And he's expected to argue?

So now the doctor has an extra baby girl. The identical twin of the one now being presented to Davis Marshall. Who needs it? Well, nobody, at the moment, but the arrangements have been made for its future use, and were in fact made six months previously. That was the day the doctor told his nurse he had confirmed to his satisfaction that twins were on the way for the Marshalls.

Twins occur once in about every eighty-six births in the United States. The odds are three to one that they won't be identical.

That was good enough odds for the wife of the third under-secretary in the Russian embassy in Washington. Her husband surprised her that day with the news that she was some three months pregnant.

Mrs. Olga Yarmolinski. For three months she wore pad-ding, increasing it gradually, confirming with a bashful smile, when eyebrows were raised on the cocktail circuit, that she was, indeed, in the family way. When she was six months preg-nant, complications arose, making it impossible for her to return, as planned, to mother Russia. She had to retire to private quarters in the Russian embassy. It was there, attended by a doctor on the embassy staff, that she gave birth to a baby girl, January 28, 1952.

It was her first child and she giggled to her husband that it was delivered by the stork. No, Olga, he said, frowning at her. You are a dirty capitalist swine Virgin Mary.

Olga Yarmolinski recovered rapidly after that. Third Undersecretary Boris Yarmolinski was soon promoted and trans-ferred back to Russia. The Yarmolinskis took their daughter with them and the immigration inspector patted the child fondly on the head as he approved their papers and passed them through the gate to their waiting aircraft. Cute little Ruskie, he thought.

In Russia the child was named Lisa Marshall. She was assigned parents who on the day of this assignment took the names of Davis and Lenore Marshall. They lived in a strange lit-tle college town in the mountains that was typically American. It had parking meters and a soda fountain and a public library and a drive-in movie and a noisy tavern and a Saturday night poker game and a newsstand where you could buy the latest copies of *Life* and *True Confessions*. It was quite a pleasant place to grow up or to attend college. The only rule they were really strict about was always speaking English. Always.

A typical and pleasant little college town named Dixon City and located in a highly restricted valley in the mountains near the Black Sea.

Everyone in Dixon City received special schooling or training of some kind, some of it quite unusual, but none as peculiar, perhaps, as that given Lisa Marshall. Her teacher kept showing her movies of herself doing things she knew she hadn't done. "That's a habit you have, isn't it, darling?" the teacher would say. "Tossing your head that way? Now, toss your head that way. That's right. *That* way...."

Once in a while a new tape would arrive. "Listen to how you say house," the teacher would say. "Isn't it funny the way you say house? You say it like a Canadian. I guess you picked that up from your Toronto friend...."

There would be strange school scribblers, too. "No, darling," the teacher would say. "You don't write an m like that. Look at how it's done in the book. You write it so...."

Most of it was a lot of fun. Getting a doll that talked for Christmas. Learning to skip rope and play hopscotch. Seeing the movies of Tom Sawyer and Bambi. Roller-skating and riding a bike and your first date and that really neat perfume and a real honest-to-God cashmere sweater....

Fun, most of it, but disappointments, too. "I'm sorry, darling," the teacher would say. "I realize you are doing very well at ballet. But you have decided that you don't like it. Don't you understand? *You* have decided..."

Disappointments and heartbreaks. "Peggy died? But she was just a baby kitten. Why would God do such a bad thing, Twerter?" Heartbreaks and shocking news. "Mom! You and Daddy? You and Daddy are getting a *divorce*...?"

Meanwhile, of course, there had been another side, very demanding and serious. Learning to speak and write Russian. Being drilled in the history of the Union of Soviet Socialist Republics. Having demonstrated beyond any doubt the perilous confrontation being provoked by the expansionistic policies of the imperialistic forces....

Finally the day came. The summer that you were twelve years old. When they took you to Moscow and you appeared before the very distinguished-looking colonel in the MVD. "Ah, so you are Lisa, eh?" the colonel had said. "It's a great privilege to meet you, my dear. Did you know you are destined to become possibly the greatest heroine in all the history of the U.S.S.R....?"

The day the colonel told you the truth. Real name Alva Kamenev. Both parents dead. Father an army officer shot and killed by a drunken GI in a much publicized incident at the Brandenburg Gate. Mother a scientist who lost her life in a tragic accident in laboratories trying to perfect a defense against germ warfare attacks...

Alva Kamenev, orphan, ward of the state, and a specially privileged young girl who, if she had the strength and the daring, could be of staggering value and service to the Union of Soviet Socialist Republics. "Now, listen carefully," the colonel had said. "Maybe many things will come clear to you now. There is, living in the United States, a girl of about your age who, by amazing coincidence..."

But that was only the start, wasn't it, young lady? Then you really had to begin a strange double life. One life was as Lisa Marshall, following, as closely as possible, the experiences of that strange girl who looked so much like you, and who—when it was important to your country—you would be called upon to replace. The other life was as Alva Kamenev, orphaned daughter of parents who died in the defense of Russia, disciplined student, dedicated communist, and youngest person ever enrolled in the top-secret Kykov Institute, major training ground for agents being groomed for subversive activities within the United States.

Friday, August 11, 1970. The switch could have been made any time after that, but it was almost surely done sometime between March 28 and September 2, 1971, the five-month period that Lisa Marshall spent in Europe. That's when the talk first started of Marshall as a possible candidate for the presidency of the United States. It also was the first time Lisa had been away from home for an extended period—the extended period that was necessary to account for the *little changes* people might notice.

"Neat, huh?" Morley smiled.

"Oh, sure," I said. "Very neat. But it's only conjecture. You can't prove it."

The smile remained. No, it said, I can't prove it, but then you can't disprove it either, can you, Charlie?

"What about the virginity bit?" I asked. "How come Alva Kamenev, Russian agent posing as Lisa Marshall, was still a virgin, *sir?* How do you explain that?"

"That's easy," Morley said. "She'd never been laid before."

"I'm serious."

"Okay," Morley said. "I'll give it to you straight. The girls in Russia don't use Tampax. Ramming those things in can really raise hell with the hymen."

I stared at him. "Why are you dodging the question?"

"Question," Morley said. "Question is as follows: Why was Alva Kamenev still a virgin when she crawled into the sack the other night with Charlie Sparrow? Answer: The Ruskies did a great job but they screwed up in this one very vital spot."

"Oh?"

"It could happen very easily," Morley said. "Look at it this way: Lisa practically grew up with Twerter. There was a very strong bond between them. Lisa could have confided to Twerter that she was a virgin and she was saving herself for Jay Edgar.

The last words the Ruskies get from Twerter is that Lisa is still a virgin. Therefore Alva Kamenev remains a virgin."

"Sure," I said. "But then Lisa starts laying around. She gets knocked up and has an abortion and…"

"Right," Morley said. "But look at your file. All this takes place in a very concentrated period. Jay Edgar was killed in mid-April, Twerter dies less than two weeks later, and Lisa has an abortion early in August. This is only a four-month period and it comes at a very bad time for the Ruskies. Twerter is dead. They are going nuts wondering if they dare try to slip another operative into the Marshall household. They are not paying that much attention at the moment to Lisa."

"They aren't?"

"If I was them, I wouldn't be," Morley said firmly. "Too much to lose and hardly anything to gain. The last thing I'd do at that stage is play around with tails on the girl. Marshall, let's remember, might be very worried about his daughter's mental attitude after the deaths of two persons so close to her, and he might have someone keeping an eye on her himself. Supposing Marshall's man spots a Ruskie tail and starts checking him out and…"

"Whoops," I said. "All those years of careful planning and preparation down the drain."

Morley nodded solemnly. "Why take that chance? Their wisest course was to keep clear and plan to make the switch at the earliest opportunity."

I had to admit he was right. The Russians would be fools to keep really close tabs. Yet close tabs were necessary to be aware of the sudden change in Lisa. While she was a very, very naughty girl, raising all kinds of hell, it did take place during only a brief period, and she did have the good sense not to make a public spectacle of herself. It took a lot of hard digging to uncover this period in her life. She'd take off, for example, for a weekend in New York, and then she'd lose herself, checking into some dump in the Village, not at the Americana. Then she'd proceed to get blasted out of her mind. Then she'd proceed to take on the whole screwing Army.

A very, very naughty girl, but only on the side streets of New York, or Newark, or maybe Baltimore. Never at home around Tuxedo Park. Not at the tennis club. Not on the eighth green of the country club.

"No," Morley was saying. "The Russians had to play it cool. No tails or other checks that might arouse the slightest suspicion. Just concentrate on getting another operative like Twerter into the Marshall household. Either get another operative in, or, what is more likely, make that damn switch …"

"Get it over with?"

"Why not?" Morley asked. "It was time for it anyway and opportunities started coming soon enough. Following her abortion, Lisa starts traveling, and now the Russians do put a watch on her, because it's a lot safer to do outside of the United States. It's not that close a watch but it is general coverage and it is noted that she's a pretty good girl. No indication that she sleeps with any of her dates."

"They think she still may be a virgin?"

"Why not?" Morley repeated. "That's the last word they got from Twerter, isn't it? They've been keeping their distance, they aren't aware of the four-month lay-around climaxed by the abortion, and now—as they pick up the trail once again—Lisa has settled down because of the abortion experience and acts like a very nice girl. Buy that?"

"Yes," I said. "But then they pull the switch. If they're careful, and they *are* careful, they are going to take a little peek, aren't they? Lisa, they find, isn't a virgin, while Alva, who is supposedly her double, is still hemmin' and hawwin' with her hymen. So then what happens?"

Morley regarded the ceiling thoughtfully. "Alva gets laid by the very distinguished colonel in the MVD. What else?"

"Which sort of screws up all your wonderful conjecture …."

"Wrong," Morley said. "You forget how devious I can be. I lied about the colonel laying Alva."

"You did?"

"Picture yourself as the Russians," Morley said. "You examine Lisa. You find evidence of a D and C, perhaps for an abortion, perhaps for other reasons. The girl very definitely isn't a virgin in a strict physical sense but she still may never have had relations with a man. So why take away Alva's virginity?"

"To play it safe."

"With whom?" Morley demanded. "Who is going to check? That's a girl's private parts. Her daddy isn't going to look and neither is her mother. She can change doctors and avoid complications there. She's a dedicated and disciplined agent and she is certainly not going to sleep around with any of Lisa's former boyfriends. If any show up, she gives them the brush, that's all, and concentrates on doing her job. So why take away her virginity? Hell, it may help, rather than hinder, in the job she has to do."

I knew the answer but I asked anyway. "How's that?"

"Supposing it is to her advantage to get married to a specific man? If she's a virgin, and she has that to offer him, it would assist her chances, wouldn't it?"

"Yeah."

Morley smiled. "Now you know why you got in so easily, don't you, Charlie?"

"Yeah, yeah…"

"You were in the moment she saw you," Morley said. "It was a perfect match. Not only could she be the daughter of the President of the United States. She also could be the wife of one of the President's closest and most trusted aides—his press secretary. Can you imagine that? Talk about a hotline between the White House and the Kremlin. Only hers would be all one-way…."

I sat staring at him.

"She even had an excuse for letting you crawl aboard immediately," Morley said. "You looked like Jay Edgar. So she went out and got herself half smashed and then she went into her ghost-from-the-past act. She had you hooked then, because not only was she beautiful, not only was she rich, not only was her daddy heading for the presidency, but she had come to you as a virgin and you had taken her under false pretenses—she was drunk and she had this crazy idea that you were Jay Edgar."

"Perfect," I said slowly. "Perfect except for one thing. I happened to be one of the few guys on the face of this earth who knew she couldn't possibly be a virgin...."

Morley was looking very pleased with himself.

"How are the chances of a trade?" I asked. "They have Lisa. We have Alva. We tell the Ruskies, nice try but..."

Morley shook his head.

"Why not?"

"Exhibit Seven," Morley said. He took another file from his briefcase and handed it to me.

It was from French Intelligence. A routine file, classified only as confidential, reporting on the death of a woman staff member of a Russian trade delegation, killed August 19, 1971, in Bordeaux. She had been found dead in the street. The apparent victim of a hit-and-run accident.

The only reason the file had been passed along by the French was that we all like to keep up to date on the status of staff members of Russian trade delegations visiting the West. This particular file, since it marked a termination, had been consigned to nowheresville, and it never would have been revived if Morley had not asked for everything—and he meant *everything*—even vaguely connected with Russian activities in Western Europe for the period March 28–September 2, 1971.

A real nothing file. Some Ruskie secretary gawking at the handsome eighteenth-century architecture gets pranged by a drunken driver. The usual attachments were stapled to it. Police reports. Eyewitness accounts. Release form. Photograph of victim. You'd have to know her to identify her from the picture.

"Lisa," I said. I handed it back.

"I'm sorry," Morley said. He dropped it on the coffee table. Now the pile of crap was a little higher.

"I mean it," he said.

Sure. He was sorry. Lisa was dead, I was sleeping with a Russian agent, and he was sorry.

Hobart looked away.

I stood up and walked into the bathroom. I let the cold tap run while I tried to think of some way out. I filled a glass with the water and drank it and then I had another glass and then I rinsed it out and then I finally gave up trying. "When are you going to arrest her?" I asked from the bathroom.

Morley didn't answer. I came out and stood at the door. Morley didn't like to talk to people unless he could see their faces.

"I'm not," he said then. "She has my blessings in her endeavors. How soon before you can pop the question?"

"You want me to marry a Russian spy?"

"Why not?" he laughed. "I've always wanted one of my agents married to one of their agents. One of my many dreams of glory."

"Useful, huh?" I said. Oh, he was looking pleased, all right. He's so God damn smart and he was looking so very, very pleased.

"Very useful," Morley said. "Let us suppose Marshall is President and you are his press secretary. Let us suppose you let it slip to your darling wife one night that we have perfected and have in operation a foolproof defense against attack by ICBM's. There may come a time, Charlie, and very soon, when a chance remark like that on your part could save the world from a nuclear holocaust...."

"Yeah," I said.

Morley got up. "She is a very pretty girl...."

"I know," I told him.

He started putting his papers and photographs back in his briefcase. "Her job will be to pump you dry. To do so she will really have to keep on your good side. You'll get a lot of loving from that pretty girl. She'll probably do anything to ..."

I lit a Viceroy with a trembling hand. "I get the picture."

"Fine," Morley said. The briefcase snapped shut. He pulled it off the table and held it primly at his side.

I went over and opened the door for him. He nodded his thanks and passed through. "Good day, gentlemen," he said. "Call me."

Oh, you are so God damn smart, Morley. So *God damn* smart....

CHAPTER TWELVE

I proposed the next morning. I hadn't planned to do it quite so soon. Marriage is a big step even if you are only marrying a Russian spy and due to the nature of her calling it is extremely unlikely that she is going to make an issue of it.

But all thought of delay vanished when Lisa rode out alone very early that morning, long before dawn, and started taking off her clothes as soon as she got inside the caravan door, leaving a trail of them on the way to the bunk.

"Good morning," she announced, down to panties and bra by the time she reached me. "My name is Lisa Marshall. I have just discovered sex. Now, move over and let us get with it."

"I have to brush my teeth," I said.

"Delays," she said. "Always delays." She pulled at the elastic on her panties and it thwacked very satisfactorily when she let it go. "I left these for you. That is right, isn't it, Charlie?"

"Yes," I said. "That is perfectly correct. Definitely proper procedure."

"I thought so," she said. "It seems to me that the man should take the girl's pants off. I mean, that sort of allows him to assert his masculinity, to demonstrate that he has the initiative in the matter, doesn't it?"

"Exactly," I said. I sat up, swung out of the bunk, and walked around her very carefully. She followed me to the sink thwacking her elastic.

"I'm learning fast, aren't I, Charlie?" she asked. The question was punctuated with an extra-loud thwack.

"You are quick," I told her. I splashed water in my face and brushed my teeth and rinsed my mouth.

"You aren't going to gargle?" Thwack.

"No," I said.

"You're sure now? It won't be that much more of a delay. If you've got a post nasal drip, all phlegmy at the back of your mouth, you can gargle if you wish, Charlie. I won't mind." Thwack.

"No drip," I said.

"Think carefully now. It's not that much more of a delay. I want to French kiss, and I've got this very long tongue, and I wouldn't want you to be embarrassed, Charlie. I wouldn't want that." Thwack.

"I am spotless," I said.

"How about shaving? That's a real five o'clock shadow you've got. Five o'clock in the morning. It doesn't take that long to shave and you know how I hate whisker burns on my tummy. What would Daddy say?" Thwack.

"I shaved last night," I said. I grabbed at her but she twisted away.

"What about a shower? I can wait, you know, and if you really…"

I got her in a corner and grabbed her and pulled her to me. She fought against me, stronger than she should be, and I almost lost her for a moment, but then she suddenly wasn't fighting any more. We stood there in the corner and kissed for a very long time.

"I love you, Charlie," she said.

"And I love you, Lisa," I told her. I took off her bra and let it drop to the floor. Her breasts were white and full and the nipples were straining with tension. I bent to kiss them.

"Don't forget this," she said. Thwack.

My mouth moved hungrily across her breasts.

"Delays," she said. "Always delays…" She pushed up against my mouth. "Charlie. *Charlie*…."

I picked her up and carried her to the bunk and lowered her gently. Her fingers were busy with the buttons of my pajamas.

"Delays," she said. She arched up at me. The soft silk panties slipped away.

"You like it, don't you, Charlie?" she whispered.

"It's okay," I said.

The first and only time I was ever in love was to a girl named Nancy Palmer, who lived upstairs over the Goodwill Store on Sherbrooke Avenue in Des Moines. I was thirteen at the time. So was she.

To demonstrate my affection I burned her name in my felt beanie cap, knocked her down and washed her face in the snow whenever the occasion permitted, and let loose a bunch of pigeons at a Girl Guide meeting she was attending in the basement of Knox United Church. When none of this worked, I filled an empty box of Crackerjack popcorn with dirty water and, during the intermission of a junior high school spring dance, poured it all over her new hairdo and the equally lovely new frock her mother had spent a week making for her.

"If," one of her girl friends observed, "he really cared for her, he wouldn't do that." Nancy apparently agreed. She never spoke to me again. Ever.

It broke my heart, of course. Destroyed my will to live. Smashed me. I swore off women until I was fifteen. It was then I discovered, rather belatedly, I suspect, a secondary use for the *glans penis,* and proceeded with all haste to compensate for the wasted years. The rest is merely history. Charlie Sparrow. Womanizer.

There was, however, only the one Nancy Palmer, and I somehow never managed to fall in love again until the night that Lisa Marshall paid her drunken visit to my caravan, calling me Jay Edgar.

That was nice. That was love. That was the real thing once more and it was trailing clouds of glory in its wake.

Only Lisa wasn't Lisa ....

So this wasn't love. It couldn't be and yet it was, damn it, and you, Morley, are a dirty, rotten, stinking, filthy, unspeakable son of a bitch, and may you burn forever in hell.

"Just okay, huh?" Lisa whispered. She pulled me down.

There is no time like the present. The world is full of signs saying, "DO IT NOW." Yet marriage is a big step even though you are only marrying a Russian spy and ...

"*Charlie,*" Lisa said. Her nails ripped at me.

"Lisa," I said. "Will you marry me?"

"Yes," she gasped.

"When?"

"Now."

"Now?"

"Charlie," she said. "*Charlie.* You know ... how I ... hate delays ...."

We had it all arranged by the time Marshall showed up on his regular morning ride, accompanied by Tyler, Sam Oppman, Maggie Hilton and two members of the palace guard at the Casa Alegre.

Marshall raised his eyebrows at Lisa. "I wondered where you had gone," he said. He seemed relieved to find her and yet he didn't look too pleased either. The others all had those glints in their eyes. Except Maggie.

Lisa pushed up off the steps and tugged me by the hand. "The early bird presents the worm," she told her father.

The eyebrows went up again.

"I'm a shameless bitch," she grinned. "I threw myself at him when he was only half awake, and it worked, too."

Marshall's face relaxed. "You two trying to tell me something?"

"Only this," Lisa said. She let go of my hand and linked her arm in mine. "Charlie has finally done the honorable thing. He proposed and I accepted. Instantly."

"Jesus Christ," Marshall said. He swung down off his bay in awkward haste and held his arms open. Lisa released me and ran to him. They embraced wordlessly.

"I'll hope you'll be very happy," Maggie told me. Her face was a mask.

"Cheers," Tyler said. He was taking it pretty well for Tyler.

Oppman looked from me to Lisa being bear-hugged by Marshall. "Well..."

The two agents were neutral but nevertheless admiring observers.

Marshall finally let go of his daughter. He strode over to me with his hand outstretched. There was just a hint of tears in his eyes. "You know how I feel. I couldn't be happier."

"Thank you," I told him. The handshake was firm and good.

"God damn it," Marshall said. He didn't seem to know what else to say. "God damn it...." He turned grinning to the others. "Would you believe this guy? One week and he steals my daughter from me. *One week!*"

Lisa laughed. "It really only took him three days...."

"There must be something in the water," Tyler said.

"No," I told him. "It's all this atom bomb testing."

"Young people," Oppman said sadly. He was still rather stunned. He looked as if he had to pay for the wedding.

"Come on in," I ordered. They piled off their horses and tied them at the hitch and tramped into the caravan for coffee. It was perked and ready.

"God damn it," Marshall kept repeating, his face all lit up, grinning at each of us in turn.

Maggie was very quiet and strained. Her presence put a real damper on me. There still was no word on what the hell she was doing in Alamos. I had the nagging fear that she had somehow been tied in with Jegalova. But if she was, she was a damn good actress, because she was giving a perfect portrayal of the woman spurned, right down to every last little detail.

"Hey," Marshall said. "I'm so excited I forgot the most important question. *When?*"

Lisa looked at me. I nodded.

"Now," she said. It was a little yelp of pleasure.

"Now?"

"Now," she repeated. "Just as soon as we can arrange it. How long does it take in Mexico?"

Marshall stared at her in disbelief. "You mean here? In Alamos?"

"Why not?"

"Well," Marshall said slowly. He looked at me and then back to Lisa. "I don't know. What about your friends? Your mother...?"

"Mom can fly down," she said. She stood and crossed to him and took his hands in hers. "Aw, come on..."

It was all so wonderfully natural, a girl in love, wheedling with her father, that there was no embarrassment in the fact that it should occur before relative strangers.

"Why not?" Marshall said at last. "Why the hell not?"

"Done!" Lisa cried. She swung back to me. "You heard him. Now you're really stuck, aren't you, mister?"

"I always was," I grinned.

Oppman sighed. "Young people..."

Maggie's hand was trembling as she raised her coffee mug to her lips. She was playing her part extremely well. But then weren't we all?

The wedding was arranged by late that afternoon. Judge Luis Esquer had agreed to perform the civil ceremony at the Casa Alegre rather than at the Palacio. It was set for noon, Thursday, February 24, with only the family and witnesses in attendance.

The reception was to follow at one o'clock at the Casa Alegre. The whole town was invited to that.

Lisa and I were to slip away in the middle of the afternoon and drive to Obregón to board Marshall's waiting Learjet. It would fly us to our honeymoon hotel in Acapulco. The Learjet, which was to arrive the previous day, bringing Lisa's mother from Philadelphia, would return that evening to Obregón. It would then take Marshall and his ex-wife back to their respective homes in New York and Philadelphia.

Lisa and I were to remain one week in Acapulco. We would then take a commercial flight to New York, where I would join Marshall's staff as he formally opened his campaign for the presidency of the United States.

"Okay," Lisa said, nodding her approval. "That fixes that. Now what do we do?" We were sitting with Marshall in his den in the Casa Alegre. She grinned at him and nodded her head toward the adjoining bedroom. "I don't suppose you'd approve if I took Charlie in there for a little premarital consorting? I could use the practice...."

Marshall reddened slightly.

"Rings," I said. "We haven't done anything about wedding rings. You know—those gold bands?"

The thought had obviously never entered her mind. "Oh, Christ, that's right," she said. She frowned in concentration. "Hey! Wait a minute. What's this gold crap? Let's settle on the diamond before we start worrying about the gold. Do you realize you haven't given me an engagement ring?"

"I'm not even sure we're engaged," I told her.

Marshall shook his head. He stood up slowly and stared down at us in turn. Then he laughed and wordlessly left the room.

Lisa jumped up as soon as the door closed. She crossed to me in four quick steps and threw herself in my lap. She put her arms around my neck and pressed her hungry mouth against mine.

"Rings," I said later.

"Yeah," she breathed. "Rings." Her hand strayed down my chest. "Will you tell me something?"

"What?"

"Do you always have this lump in your pants?"

We purchased two very plain gold bands at the gift shop at the Casa de los Tesoros. Neither fit properly, but they were the only two they had, and we didn't much give a damn anyway, we told the clerk. The shop didn't have any diamond rings and it was unlikely there would be much of a choice in either Navojoa or Obregón.

"So who cares?" Lisa demanded. "We'll get engaged after we get married. Okay?"

"Doesn't everybody?" I asked.

The clerk was also laughing and shaking her head by the time we left Two young lovers. Playing our parts extremely well.

I left Alamos very early the next morning to drive the caravan back across the border at Nogales. I had brought it into Mexico, and the rules said I had to take it out, not somebody else. While it was possible to make other arrangements, I needed to get away by myself, to do some serious thinking, and so I grabbed at the excuse. Everything had been happening too damn fast. Too quick.

Lisa kissed me good-bye tearfully. The tears seemed terribly real and honest. "Damn you," she said.

"I'll be back early Wednesday," I promised.

"You better be," she said. "The wedding is Thursday. Remember?"

I nodded solemnly. It wasn't something I was likely to forget.

Lisa made a sucking noise in the corner of her mouth. "Okay. Bugger off. If you don't get the hell out of here, you're going to see some real tears, mister."

I tousled the hair the color of ripe bananas. "Good-bye," I said.

I left her standing like a lost and forlorn puppy in front of the Casa Alegre.

It is exactly a 400-mile drive from Alamos to Nogales. Except for the short stretch into Navojoa, it's all on Mexico's Highway 15, the Gulf of California coastal route, so-called, between Arizona and Mexico City. North from Navojoa there are only three places of any size, Ciudad Obregón, Guaymas, the famous deep-sea fishing port on the gulf, and then Hermosillo, the capital of Sonora. Guaymas is the only place where the highway actually runs alongside the gulf.

Most of the way it is pretty much down in the flatlands, entirely different from the foothills country of Alamos, although mountains are visible, and often quite near, over much of the route. There also are stretches of irrigated fields from time to time that relieve the monotony of the winter desert.

The caravan, as I've said, was built for comfort, not speed, and it took me almost ten hours to make the trip. I left at six in the morning and made it across the border just before four that afternoon. But to do even that well I had to pass up a lunch stop.

I checked in, as arranged, at the Trail Rider Motel in Nogales, phoned immediately to confirm my charter flight back to Alamos early Wednesday, and then headed for a much needed shower. I had just finished when there was a knock at the door. I wrapped a towel around myself and padded across the carpet to open it.

"Surprise," Maggie Hilton said. Or was it Doris Dubois? I could never be quite sure. Maybe she really was the younger Lana Turner.

I hitched up my towel and stood staring at her.

"May I come in?"

"Sure," I said. "What did you do? Hide under the bunk?"

She laughed. "Are you kidding? I flew up this afternoon. I've had quite enough of your stupid caravan."

"Oh?"

She dropped exhausted into a chair. "Yup. But we're so short-handed—they want me to dump it off in Tucson."

"You don't say...."

"Yup," she repeated. She held out her hand with the palm up. "Give them to me. I want to spend the night there. Civilization—*at last.*"

"Them...?"

"The keys," she said. "You know the kind? They unlock doors and turn on ignitions. Keys. K-e-y-s."

"Oh," I said. I had the distinct impression that my lower jaw was somewhere near the floor. I pulled it back into place with considerable effort.

"You're kidding," she said.

I shook my head.

"Oh, Jesus," she laughed. "That damn Morley. You mean he hasn't told you yet?"

"Who?"

She laughed again, opened her purse, and withdrew a voice scrambler. She set it on the table in front of her. It was a real one and it was operating.

"The keys," she repeated.

I went to the closet and got them out of my jacket pocket. She must have seen the look on my face as they came flying across the room.

"I'm sorry," she said. "Maybe it isn't quite that funny. But I did need a laugh."

"Don't we all?" I said. I grabbed some underwear and a pair of slacks and slammed into the bathroom. I heard her leave while I was pulling on the slacks. That made me even angrier.

I came back out, stared for a long time at the chair she had just vacated, and then shrugged and took a bottle of Old Crow out of my suitcase. I poured a couple of fingers in a glass and downed it straight. Doris Dubois. Jesus.

Morley's mind works like that. Maggie had been Tyler's opposite. Tyler was supposed to be the competition in my quest for Lisa. Maggie was supposed to be Lisa's competition if she showed any interest in me. Never underestimate the value of competition. It whets your appetite. It makes you eager.

For it to really work, I couldn't be in on the gag, and just to make sure I didn't get any wild ideas about trying to play around on the side with Maggie, they had waited until just the right moment—until Lisa's arrival in Alamos—to feed me the phony file about the mysterious Doris Dubois. That's all it took to guarantee hands off.

Maggie Hilton. The mysterious Doris Dubois. The younger Lana Turner. There had been moments, in the early stages, when I had considered bedding her, and now she was long gone. She had taken my keys and she had stolen off into the night. She had left when I was pulling *on* my pants. How about that? Good-bye, farewell, and so long....

I regarded the bottle of Old Crow. Perhaps another couple of fingers would do nicely before dinner. A couple three fingers or maybe even a home run. I reached for the bottle and the telephone rang. My hand changed course.

"Why don't you drop over?" Morley suggested.

"Where is over?" I asked. He sounded next-door.

"Next-door," Morley said.

I had the room at the end of the balcony on the second floor of the north wing. There was only the one next-door. It took me about five seconds. Then I was rapping.

"It's open," Morley said.

I let myself in. The room was an exact duplicate of mine. Motel modern and only one decent easy chair. Morley was not occupying it. That meant the man who was sitting there had to be something special. Higher than Morley.

"Sit down," Morley said. His hand motioned to the one vacant chair left in a semicircle around the cheap plastic-topped coffee table. I joined the party—Morley, Hobart and Something Special.

I eyed Hobart. It must have been him who had flown Maggie to Nogales. The bastard could have prepared me for when she came knocking at the door ....

"I hear you got engaged this morning," Morley said.

"You've been misinformed," I told him. "We're not getting engaged until after we are married. There is a shortage of suitable diamond rings in Mexico. What is required is large." I held up my fist. "Like so. Do you think the budget can stand it?"

Morley smiled thinly. "I'm glad you delayed the purchase."

"Oh?"

His eyes moved imperceptibly to Something Special. "There isn't going to be any wedding."

"Oh?" I said again. There was suddenly a very hard knot in my stomach.

"Change of plans," Morley said agreeably. "It seems I have been overruled. The chosen few who constitute the review board in these matters have decided that it would not be such a good idea after all if we permitted a Russian spy to be part of the First Family."

"Now you tell me," I said. The words didn't come out the way I had intended. The desired flippancy was missing. Entirely.

"He was informed only recently himself," Something Special said. The tone of his voice added that there would be no further discussion of this aspect.

I sat back and waited.

"It goes this way," Morley said. "Marshall is one of the few candidates of any stature left on the scene. The incumbent has no objections to Marshall's candidacy. Rather he considers him likely timber—minus the pretty lady from the Kykov Institute. The Secretary of State and the Defense Secretary are in agreement ...."

I nodded and the knot tightened.

"This presents a problem," Morley said. "You do see the difficulty? How do we get rid of Lisa and not scuttle Marshall's chances of being elected?"

I looked at Something Special. His face was a complete blank. Empty.

"We can't very well arrest the girl," Morley went on. "If we did that, we'd have to charge her with espionage, of course, and you can imagine a man's chances of being elected President if his daughter—even one kidnapped at birth—is being held as a spy. His chances of being elected would be zero."

I turned back to face him.

"So," Morley said. He spread the fingers of his hands. They moved apart slowly along the edge of the coffee table.

"Say it," I told him.

He raised his eyes to mine. "There is no other way...."

"Say it."

"Very well," Morley said. "Tomorrow afternoon yet another attempt will be made to assassinate Marshall. This one also will fail. Marshall will escape unharmed. But Lisa..."

The knot in my stomach burst.

"I am sorry," Morley was saying. "If you wish, you needn't be there, of course. You can phone her tomorrow morning and make some excuse. Tell her you've run into problems and you will be back in the afternoon." He turned and silently asked permission from Something Special. "Tell her you'll meet her at three o'clock at the Casa Alegre."

Now, wasn't that awfully nice of him? If I wished, I needn't be there, of course. "You're being a little rough, aren't you?" I said.

"It's a rough game," Something Special said. He examined his left hand as if expecting to find a hangnail. Actually he was examining me.

Game. Why did everybody call it a game?

"We've considered this from every possible aspect," Morley said. "The decision has been made. The girl has to be removed.

Unfortunately, we are not equipped to keep her on ice for four to eight years, as is possible in the country that trained her so effectively...."

"I know that," I said. Wonderful excuse. We had no political prison. We couldn't toss someone in a secret jail without benefit of counsel and public trial. We had to go by the book and so, in a situation such as this, which the book simply didn't cover, we had to toss the book away. We had to kill her.

"Mexico is an ideal place to do it," Morley said. "Especially Alamos. The federal police there are cupcakes. They've never fired a shot in anger. Hobart says they haven't even got cars."

"It's a quiet town," I said.

"We're going to make this look very professional," Morley said. "Three men in the hit. Commando stuff, lots of lead flying, gas all over the place and ..."

"Gas?"

Morley nodded. "Your excuse. You'll get a canister in your lap. No permanent harm but you'll be out cold for at least an hour."

"Lisa," I said. "When they do it to her ..." My eyes strayed to Something Special. "How?"

"A bullet," Morley said. "The man assigned is an expert. He knows how close and what part of the brain and she'll be dead before she hits the floor."

"Quick," Something Special said.

Sure. My Lisa. Exquisite. Very, very sexy. And quick.

"It's up to you," Morley said. "You don't have to be there. You can stay or go back as planned. But if you do go back, you'll have to set her up for us, of course. Make sure she's at the casa when the hit is made."

Of course.

"Can you do that?" Something Special asked.

"Yes," I said. "When? Three o'clock?"

He nodded solemnly.

"Then it's all arranged," Morley said with relief. He looked at me for a moment. "Hobart is leaving shortly for Obregón. Do you want to go back tonight?"

He was being so awfully nice. One last night. Once more.

"No," I said.

CHAPTER THIRTEEN

"I can't believe it," Lisa said. The deep green eyes mirrored her utter disbelief.

"It's true," I told her, kissing her nose. "If you can't cook, it's all off, baby. So get your bottom in that kitchen and cook me some breakfast. Personally."

"Huh," she said.

I turned her around, patted the aforementioned bottom, and sent her off in the direction of the kitchen. First, she had her shoulders squared, pretending to be angry, but when she couldn't carry that off, she started rolling her hips exaggeratedly. The sexpot venturing into the unknown. Lesson 436B at the Kykov Institute.

Sweet Mother of Jesus, I prayed. Please save us. Please save us all.

I sat down at a wrought-iron table with a glass top at the edge of the swimming pool. Across the water, a member of the palace guard, who would be a witness when the yellow hair ran with blood, looked away from me self-consciously. And what, I wondered, staring at his averted profile, are your secret thoughts this morning? What is your considered opinion of Charlie Sparrow?

He must have been aware of my attention. In a moment he stood up and crossed to another chair behind a palm. Out of sight, out of mind, huh? Or something.

I looked at my watch. It was just after ten. Five hours to go ....

Set her up, Morley had said, and she was set, ready and waiting. I had arrived half an hour before at the Casa Alegre. Yes,

Lisa had whispered, when the tender kisses were done, it would be fun to spend the day at the house, just loafing around the pool, baking in the sun. Yes, Marshall had agreed, when the old hug and handshake were over, if you want to have a little chat this afternoon, some time around three, just after siesta, would be fine and dandy.

No problem. Listen, you heard that, did you, Something Special? No problem. No problem at all.

I tried to think of something else. I took one of my Viceroys, lit it, puffed a couple of times, and then snubbed it out. Could she cook? Was that one of the things they taught you at the Kykov Institute?

There was a folded newspaper on the chair beside me. I reached for it absently and spread it open on the table. It was the front section of a week-old copy of the New York *Times.* "Israeli Commandos Hit Beirut Airport," the headline stated.

I read the story without it really registering on me. Middle East closer to war than at any time since hostilities formally ceased.... Diplomats of the U.S., Russia, Britain and France meeting in three capitals to discuss crisis.... Washington judges Middle East the one place right now where a confrontation with the Russians could occur....

A door opened behind me. "Did you say over?"

"Gently," I said.

The door closed.

I went back to the New York *Times.* The great importance of monetary policy has been demonstrated lately by the stock market.... U.S. Army forces simulated nuclear attacks today in war games being staged on maneuver grounds thirty miles from Soviet-occupied Czechoslovakia.... There are few countries in the world which wish to remain a colony—but the sultanate of Brunei, on the north coast of Borneo, is one of them....

The door opened. "How gently?"

I turned to face her. She was walking toward me with a tray laden with my breakfast. By the look on her face, it was going to be very, very good.

"Fresh-squeezed," she said, placing the orange juice on the table. "Eggs over, gently. Bacon, crisp. Coffee, black."

"Toast," I said. "You forgot the toast."

A hunk of yellow hair passed before her eyes. "Uh, uh. That gets made here. I'll be right back...."

I drank the orange juice. It was freshly squeezed, all right, and the oranges were just off the tree, but it was still like drinking gall. It is not true what they say. The condemned man does not eat a hearty breakfast.

"My specialty," Lisa said, setting a toaster and four slices of bread on the table. "Sour dough. *Extra* sour dough." She plugged the toaster in an outlet on the patio floor and dropped two pieces of bread into place with the exactness of a little girl playing house. "You are going to love sour dough toast."

"I am?"

"You are."

She sat down across from me and poured herself a cup of coffee. "You know what this is?"

"Coffee."

"No," she said. "It's our first breakfast together. An historic occasion. A milestone."

"Do you think they will erect a roadside marker?"

She nodded solemnly. "Definitely. Very definitely."

I tried the coffee.

"Wait a minute," she said. "This isn't right." She reached for the discarded front section of the New York *Times*. "Here. Let's not start off on the wrong foot. You've *got* to be reading the paper...."

"You're sure?"

"Positive," she said. "I want our marriage to last. If we begin with you not reading the paper at breakfast, and then, a year from now, you start reading it—well, that would blow the deal sky high, wouldn't it, Charlie?"

"Probably."

"You know it," she grinned. "I can just hear myself. What's the matter? Why don't you ever talk to me anymore? Don't you love me ... ?"

I had the paper up in front of my face. "I'll always love you," I said.

"Does it say that in the New York *Times?*"

"No. It says, 'Israeli Commandos Hit Beirut Airport.' "

"That poor airport. It's getting the hell beat out of it. What else?"

I read a few more headlines. There was no reply. I glanced over the paper at her. She seemed totally preoccupied buttering the toast.

"Pope Raps War," I said.

"Yea, Pope," she said.

I returned to the truth. "Earl Harkley is dead," I said.

Lisa's attention remained focused on the toast. "That's news?"

Perhaps not, I admitted to myself. In my opinion, he'd been dead for years—from the neck up. I looked for something else of more interest.

"May 14," Lisa said proudly. "I remember the date exactly. Friday, May 14, 1971."

"The date of what?"

"The day he died, silly. I was living in Paris at the time and I remember it exactly."

"You do, huh?"

"Sure," Lisa said. "I was having lunch with this boy I'd met, Bryce Hamilton, a real socialist fink, when he saw it in the papers, and then we got into this enormous argument."

"An argument?"

"A war, practically. He thought Earl Harkley was the greatest invention since the sanitary napkin. I thought—well, we had this war, and he didn't take me out that night as promised, and I missed a really super party at the Ecole des Beaux Arts. Friday, May 14, 1971. I'll never forget it."

Very interesting. It was Wednesday, February 23, 1972, I was reading a week-old copy of the New York *Times,* and on the front page—a two-column story above the fold—it stated very positively that James Benjamin Rumsey Harkley, 3d Earl Harkley, had died the previous night, in Westmorland in the north of England.

"Why are you looking at me so funny?"

There was no hiding the story. I had to show it to her. I folded the paper and passed it across the table. "Read that," I said, pointing.

Her face flushed and she managed an imitation smile. "Well," she said carefully. "How do you like that? I guess it must have been a different earl...."

"Women," I grinned. "They can be so *positive* about something."

She stuck her tongue out. "Men," she said.

After breakfast I made an excuse about wanting to buy a gift at the Casa de los Tesoros. She gave me a kiss and the keys to her car and I drove there with my heart pumping wildly. I put in a call to CI-2 Research in Washington and explained the situation to Marnie. She said to do it properly would take at least a couple of hours. I told her to very definitely do it in less than that and to call me back.

The call didn't come until almost noon. By that time I had gone through half a pack of cigarettes.

"How do you want this?" Marnie asked.

"I'm not sure I do," I said.

"Briefly," Marnie said. "This was a boo-boo by the East German news agency. They mistakenly reported the death of Earl Harkley, May 14, 1971. But they put out a correction almost immediately and as far as I can determine the only place the story ran was in one edition of Zurich's *Neue Zürcher Zeitung.*"

"Zurich?"

"Yes," Marnie said. "That's in Switzerland. Maybe you have heard of it. They have Alps and stuff."

"How would the East German news agency make a mistake like that?"

"I don't know," Marnie said. "I called and asked and they told me to get stuffed. But I have a guess."

"Tell me your guess."

"I really did call Appleby," Marnie said. "I was on the line forever. The British are getting so impossible these days."

"The results, please."

"Well," Marnie said. "On May 14, 1971, the Appleby *News and Market,* circulation 3,840, had its first stop-press news story in years. It carried a one-paragraph bulletin reporting the death of Earl Harkley."

"It did, huh?"

"Yes," Marnie said. "Only not James Benjamin Rumsey Harkley, 3d Earl Harkley, philosopher, mathematician, author and pinko. This was just plain Earl Harkley. That was his first name. Earl."

"But a big man in his own right in Appleby?"

"I'll say," Marnie said. "He owned half the countryside. Dairy farming. Cattle raising. Quoth the bulletin: 'Earl Harkley, Westmorland's leading citizen, passed away today, of an apparent heart seizure, at the family estate, Lamont Castle, the chief constable reports.' "

"The East German news agency had a correspondent in England?"

"Two," Marnie said. "At this particular time it had two. The regular man was based on Fleet Street plus a man on special assignment from East Berlin. The latter was touring England writing a series of articles entitled 'Decline of the Lion.' And on this date he was poking around Westmorland."

It all started to fall into place for me. "So he read the bulletin in the *News and Market,* put in a quick call to his office in

East Berlin, reported the death of one of the West's most famous fellow-travellers, and then phoned the chief constable for more details and discovered his blunder. The British are so impossible. They have two kinds of Earls ...."

"I guess," Marnie said. "The East German news agency would have the mistake on the wire for maybe half an hour before sending out a correction. *Neue Zürcher Zeitung* was the only client that got caught. One lousy edition."

"Which one?"

"The first," Marnie said. "The story was pulled for the second. That and subsequent editions carried a small correction."

"Where is the first edition circulated?"

"In the East," Marnie said. "*Neue Zürcher Zeitung* has two international editions. The first goes East and the final goes West. How do you think the Swiss have managed to remain neutral all these years?"

"Did the correction run in the first edition of the following day?"

"Noop," Marnie said. "Sloppy, huh? The most individual, the most serious, the most responsible and the most cosmopolitan of the elite press of the world. From its lofty pinnacle in its neutral and freedom-loving country, it views all the world with a cold and intellectual detachment, but it can get sloppy, huh?"

"The first edition definitely doesn't circulate in France?"

"Doesn't," Marnie said. "It goes to Eastern Europe. Behind the Iron Curtain. Maybe you have heard of it. They have this curtain, see, and it is made of iron, and ..."

"I love you."

"Don't I wish," Marnie said.

I hung up and made another call. This one to a guy I once did a big article on for *Look*. He's a doctor who specializes in cases of patients in deep comas. Dr. Philip Saarlander, and the reason for the article was that he had been brought in on a supposedly hopeless case, a young traffic accident victim who had been in a coma for more than two years, and he had succeeded in reviving the boy.

Luckily, he remembered my name, and I got through to him right away at his office in Boston, and when I explained the situation to him he said it was possible—*entirely possible*. I thanked him and then I made one more call. To Morley.

I told him all about my breakfast conversation with Lisa, and the research done by Marnie, and the expert opinion expressed by Saarlander.

"Conjecture," Morley said.

"You are human," I said. "You are capable of error. It is possible for you to make a mistake, *sir*."

"Think up some excuse," Morley said. "Get the hell out of Alamos. Just be sure you are always with someone—a nice, safe, responsible, independent witness. Get the hell out of the way for the rest of the day and by the time you come back it will be all over."

"For Christ's sake," I said. "Can't you admit you made a mistake? You were right all along except that you made a mistake about when they pulled the switch. They pulled it right after Jay Edgar got killed in Viet Nam."

"I don't think so."

"Yes," I said. "Look at the file. Lisa was all broken up. She wanted to be alone. She took off for Marshall's summer place on the Hudson. She spent three days alone there and then the girl who came back wasn't Lisa—it was Alva."

"It had to be done during an *extended* absence."

"No," I said. "It was done during a brief period of shock and depression. The girl who came back was different, changed, and why shouldn't she be, eh? Her fiancé had been killed."

"I'm not going to argue…"

"You are, damn it. Look at the file. Twerter was dead within a week. Heart attack? Like hell. She was killed by an expert. A communist agent who, once she got inside the Marshall household, realized that it wasn't just an amazing coincidence that she looked so much like Lisa, but that she was in fact the identical twin sister of Lisa, the natural-born daughter of the man she was sent to spy on."

"Then why wouldn't she tell her father or go to the police or the FBI?"

"Because she had killed Twerter. I don't know how it happened, but the moment she discovered the truth, Twerter was there, part of the apparatus, the one thing she could strike out at, and she did strike out and she did kill and then she didn't know where to turn next."

"Conjecture."

"Damn you," I said. "Look at the file. It all fits. Alva makes Twerter's death look like a heart attack, to us, to the Ruskies. She decides she can't turn to us. Would we believe her in the first place? Would she be sent to jail or executed for Twerter's murder? The only thing she can do is keep playing along, praying that Marshall won't become President, hoping against hope that she'll never be placed in the position where she'll have access to secrets from the White House."

Morley laughed. "That's hardly a favor for Marshall. If Marshall doesn't become President, he's dead, and so is his ex-wife. The Russians will kill both of them and go after the prize they were after in the first place. Just one inheritance and they've caught up with us in electronics and have access to all the secrets of one of the country's biggest defense contractors...."

"No," I said. "This is bigger than that. It always has been. Can't you understand? The Bordeaux 'accident' was a fake. *Neither* of the girls are dead. They were simply switched around again. The Ruskies have Alva, they are getting her back into shape, and when the time comes..."

"Conjecture."

"Keep saying that," I said. "Just keep on saying it. But it was Alva, not Lisa, who started drinking and laying around, Morley. It was Alva who got knocked up, and who got an abortion, and who went on the run, and who finally had to be pranged in Bordeaux. It was Alva who 'died' on that side street and it was Lisa who came back home to America."

Morley sighed. "All right. It's not conjecture. It's just damn nonsense."

"No," I said. "Call Saarlander. Ask him. Ask him and he will tell you. It is possible—*entirely possible.* The Russians didn't kill Lisa. They simply drugged her and smuggled her out of the country. They took her to some clinic in Eastern Europe and they kept her in a deep coma and they created a continuing life for her with the use of drugs and hypnosis and auto-suggestion and all that kind of crap you know damn well they are so far ahead of us in, and then ..."

"Damn nonsense."

I was begging him now. "Call Saarlander. Ask him and ask other experts. It is *entirely possible.* You can keep a person in a coma and you can create a continuing life for them. You can tell them under hypnosis that certain things are happening to them and when they wake up they will believe that these things actually did happen. You can tell a person: Today is Friday, May 14, 1971. It is another beautiful day for your visit to Paris. You are having lunch with the boy you've met, Bryce Hamilton, the young socialist, the one who is going to take you out tonight, to the party at the Ecole des Beaux Arts. But what's this news in today's newspaper? Earl Harkley has died. Bryce Hamilton thinks so much of Earl Harkley ...."

"Stop it!"

"I won't," I said. "Can't you see how it happened? Lisa was being kept in a coma and they were creating a life for her by weaving imaginary events around the world's day-to-day news as reported in the first edition of *Neue Zürcher Zeitung.* The major news events of each day were being talked into her mind the same way you'd talk them into a tape recorder. This way, if it ever became necessary to revive her, to switch her back with Alva, she would have a *complete memory* of a *normal life* during the whole period she was in a coma."

"Why would they want to switch back?"

"How do I know?" I demanded. "For any number of possible reasons. Supposing Alva couldn't hack it? Supposing they just made the switch, and Alva started cracking up under the pressure, and they had to pull her out for a while, give her a rest and a pep talk? Wouldn't it ease their minds to be able to switch back and forth ... ?"

Morley laughed. "I've just thought of a new television series. 'The Interchangeables.' "

"Why don't you admit it?" I asked. "Everything I've told you is possible. Entirely possible."

There was a long silence. My knuckles were chalk white from my grip on the phone.

"Perhaps," Morley said finally. "I think you've finally convinced me. The key to the whole thing is the false story of Earl Harkley's death that appeared in just the one edition of *Neue Zürcher Zeitung.* They implanted the fact of Earl Harkley's death in Lisa's mind and then never erased it with a correction ... ?"

"Right," I breathed.

"I can see how it might happen," Morley said. "*Neue Zürcher Zeitung* didn't print a correction the next day. The doctor who is creating Lisa's continuing life goes blithely along thinking Earl Harkley really did die. It might be weeks or months before he learns otherwise and by that time perhaps he has forgotten that this death is one of the facts he has implanted. Or maybe there are several doctors involved and one assumes the other made the correction and it sort of gets lost in the shuffle ... ."

"It's possible."

"Well," Morley said. "That was a close call. If you hadn't been reading the New York *Times* at breakfast ..."

I didn't have the strength left to reply.

"We've got to think this out," Morley said. "We've got to sit down together and think this all out again. Is Hobart around?"

"No."

"Find him," Morley said. "Find him and have him call me. Okay?"

"Okay," I said. "And thanks...."

Morley laughed. "*Thank you.*"

He hung up and I cursed myself. There was one other argument to bolster my cause. Billie's dying words, when I mentioned Marshall, had been "Beautiful, simply beautiful...."

Who was simply beautiful? Alva, of course, and she had been down to Easter, carefully avoiding the police, poking into the early life of her father, vainly trying to locate some old friend or relative who might be able to prove her belief that she was the identical twin of Lisa. The belief had driven her to strike out and kill in an unthinking rage, and then, when she wanted solid evidence to prove her belief, she had gone looking for it in Easter. She was awfully careful, she avoided the police, she missed Agnes, but she did look up people in the old folks home at Valentine. A vain search that would find nothing. There was nothing to find.

That was why Ace King had followed me to Easter. That was why he had killed Agnes, and tried to kill me, and then doubled back to kidnap Billie, to take her away and kill her, too. Ace King wasn't worried about what I might discover about Marshall. His worry was that I might learn Alva had been asking questions around Easter. If I learned she had been there, and she had been asking questions, and the *kind of questions* she had been asking ...

I went into the hotel bar and had a good stiff drink of whisky. Then I went back into the lobby and stood around thumbing through the magazines until the switchboard girl wasn't looking my way. There was a door at the rear of the lobby leading to the telephone circuits. I'd been in there before, looking over the equipment, checking for taps, and so it only took me a minute. When I came back through the door the hotel's switchboard was out of commission for at least a day. Fifteen minutes and two hotels later and there wasn't a telephone operating in all Alamos.

Lisa was waiting impatiently when I finally got back to the Casa Alegre.

"You are a wanderer," she said.

"I know," I told her. "Answer me a question?"

"What?"

"Remember the summer you spent in Paris?"

She grinned. "No one forgets Paris."

"Seriously," I said. "Did anything happen to you while you were there? Did you get hurt or something and have to spend a bit of time in the hospital?"

The grin was exchanged for a funny look. "Why?"

"I'm just asking."

"All right," she said. "I'm telling you but no one else. It's our secret. Right?"

"Right."

"I apparently got involved in one hell of a traffic accident."

"Apparently?"

She made a face. "That's what I said—*apparently.* I woke up in this little private clinic somewhere outside of Bordeaux. The doctor told me I had been out like a light for two whole days."

"You couldn't remember the accident?"

"No, but I saw my car later, and it was lucky I only got a bump on the head, I'm telling you."

"You didn't suffer any other loss of memory?"

"No. Just the opposite. I remember a lot of things with an awful clarity. It's as if…" She made that face again. "Why do you ask?"

I shrugged. "I'm just curious. I want to know all about you, that's all. Did you ever tell your father or mother?" "No. The doctor at the clinic said they hadn't been able to locate my parents. I thought, what the heck, I'm okay, so why worry them for nothing? You know what parents are like. I didn't let them know at the time and when I got home I just kept my mouth shut...."

"This clinic. Think you could find it again?"

"Whatever for?"

"Could you?"

She frowned. "Maybe. When I regained consciousness, the doctor phoned the police, and this plainclothes officer showed up to question me, and then—since I was being released—he volunteered to drive me into Bordeaux. It was at night and it was way out in the woods somewhere and ..."

"Never mind," I said. "Do you trust me?"

There was no frown now. "Only with my life."

"Thank you," I said. "What say we go for a ride? Right now."

There are several back roads out of Alamos. I took the old Camino Real, heading south, and that was the worst possible choice, but it didn't really matter. They had us blocked every way.

Two miles out of town there was a pickup truck sitting crossways. I didn't see it until I rounded a bend and when I glanced in the rear-view mirror at the same instant there was a cloud of dust coming up behind. There was nothing to do but to stop. Too many men. Too many guns.

Hobart got out of the truck and walked over to my side of the car.

"You've got to listen," I told him.

"Sure, kid," Hobart said. He motioned to a couple of agents and they moved in on the other side to take Lisa.

I bent my wrist and the cylinder dropped down into my palm.

"Don't," Hobart said. He was very fast with his pistol. It was two inches from my skull.

"Charlie," Lisa said.

I sat there in silence until I saw that they were taking her around the pickup truck and I realized that there was another car waiting on the other side and it was going to be heading south. They weren't taking her back to Alamos. They were taking her someplace else. Away.

"You're making a mistake," I said.

"We all make mistakes, kid," Hobart said. "Your mistake was to fall in love. Your mistake was to ..."

"Charlie," Lisa screamed. "Charlie, for God's sake, *please ...*"

"Don't," Hobart said. He pushed the pistol against my temple.

That Morley. That dirty, stupid, ignorant ...

"You of all people," Hobart said. "You of all people had to go fall in love. Don't you know the old saying—love is blind?"

Sure. Love is blind. It is blind and it can also be good. Very, very good. Nice.

"I have to hand it to you, though," Hobart said. "You were cute. Really cute. Imagine anybody remembering that *Neue Zürcher Zeitung* once mistakenly reported the death of Earl Harkley? Imagine filing away a crazy piece of information like that and then being able to use it to your advantage almost a year later when you want to save the life of a little Commie pussy ...?"

Save the life? Oh, Jesus Christ, Morley. Jesus Christ ....

"Cute," Hobart said. "Really cute. That must have been something when you told her you were an agent, and that you knew she was an agent, too. I can just see the shock on that pretty face and then the relief when you offered her the way out. What sort of story did you two cook up? That she woke up in this strange little hospital? That she could remember everything except ..."

Lisa's scream was muffled.

"Pull it," I said. "Do me this one last favor, will you, Hobart? Pull the trigger."

He pushed the pistol until it was cutting into the flesh.

"If you kill that girl, you kill me, Hobart," I said. "I'll go nuts if you kill that girl so you might as well kill me. Pull the trigger. Please."

Hobart laughed. "You'll recover, kid," he said.

CHAPTER FOURTEEN

Special privilege tonight. They let me have a radio. The only thing, the nurse said, is I've got to keep it under my pillow, hidden from the others, and I can only use the ear plug, not turn it on for real. I can see her point. The others need their rest. Their undisturbed rest.

I wish I could get some undisturbed rest. I keep having these terrible dreams. They are always about a new television series called "The Interchangeables." There's this kid, Davis Marshall, who grows up on an isolated ranch, and when his parents die and he goes out into the big wide world, the Ruskies grab him and substitute an agent in his place. The substitute is a bit older—*big for his age,* somebody said—and after he establishes a boyhood for himself by going to school a couple of years, he goes to work in the oil fields, then joins the Army, then completes college, then becomes a very big success in the business world.

He can't miss being a success. The Ruskies give him an unlimited supply of money to invest in various businesses. They've also got all kinds of electronic experts busy as hell back in Russia supplying him with the designs and p-p-p-patents that make his the leading electronics firm in all the United States ....

I'm glad they let me have the radio. The election returns are coming in hot and heavy now. Marshall just picked up Illinois and he is leading in Texas. That's his birthplace and so he is pretty sure to take the old Lone Star.

This damn dream. The Ruskies have a huge investment to protect. They keep an awfully close watch on their man. When they learn his wife is going to have twins, they take one away at birth, train her as an agent, and then make a switch as their man starts heading towards the White House. Why not? Why not be doubly sure? Why not take out an insurance policy on that huge investment?

The stakes, after all, are only complete world domination, and if your man should ever start getting second thoughts, it's not a bad idea to have one of his daughters as a hostage and the other looking over his shoulder, watching his every move. It's not a bad idea to have an insurance policy even if you are not asking that much of your man.

You're not asking him to destroy America. You're not asking him to refuse to give the order for counterattack when the ICBM's start raining down on New York and Chicago and Los Angeles. You might, of course, if it ever came to that, but basically all you want him to do is load his Cabinet with communists, and get rid of as many good guys as possible in the government, and sign a nuclear disarmament pact that favors Russia, and cut back very sharply on the nation's defenses, and not make a stink when the Ruskies really start taking over other countries, and spend four years weakening the whole structure, screwing the economy, causing widespread unemployment, sowing more unrest among the Negroes, provoking...

It's official now. Marshall won in Texas. The CBS computer says he's got it made if he can swing California. Swing it? Hell, look how well he did there in the p-p-p-primary, will you? He did damn well then and it wasn't all sympathy vote. The voters felt sorry, sure, him losing his only d-d-d....—his only child in that tragic auto accident, but it wasn't all sympathy, CBS computer.

What a crazy dream. Morley would get a really big kick out of it. There's such an obvious hole. Willard Sutton, fourth-generation American, chairman of the Board of Oil America, would have to be in on the plot. Sutton owes his all to the United States. He started with just a couple of lousy oil fields and now he's one of the richest men in America. He owes everything he has to the old free enterprise system. Besides, who ever heard of a d-d-d-disloyal fourth-generation American...?

First returns from California. Marshall well in the lead. That does it, I guess. Our next President.

That damn Morley. He promised to visit me and he has never showed. When he does, I've got this really cute question for him, if I can just remember it. Here's how it goes: Listen, Morley, if Marshall grew up on a ranch, how come he's such a l-l-lousy rider, *sir?*

If I can just remember it, I'm going to ask him that question, because I'm sure he'll have this really sharp answer. You know Morley. He's so G-G-God damn s-s-smart....

Made in the USA
Columbia, SC
18 August 2021

THEIR MAN IN THE WHITE HOUSE

Also by Tom Ardies

Kosygin is Coming (aka Russian Roulette)
In a Lady's Service
Palm Springs

The Charlie Sparrow Series

Their Man in the White House
This Suitcase is Going to Explode
Pandemic

As Jack Trolley

Balboa Firefly
Manila Time
Juarez Justice
La Jolla Spindrift

As Richard O'Brien

Storming Heaven
By Friends Betrayed

THEIR MAN IN
THE WHITE HOUSE

TOM ARDIES

ISBN-13: 978-1-7358517-5-4

Published by
Brash Books
PO Box 8212
Calabasas, CA 91372
www.brash-books.com